Contents

Introduction

Storm Constantine

In 2013, Tanith Lee – one of the world's most talented writers of fantasy, as well as of other genres – was presented with a Lifetime Achievement award at the World Fantasycon convention, which was held that year in Brighton in the UK. To commemorate this event, Tanith asked Immanion Press to publish a limited edition collection of her short stories in hardback – just 30 copies – which would be available only at the convention. The book would be called 'Animate Objects'. As she states on the cover text, Tanith believed 'there is no such thing as an inanimate object', and explores this idea in her introduction to this collection, giving insight as to why she wrote these tales, and the inspirations behind them.

As you'd expect, once news of 'Animate Objects' reached Tanith's fans, many were eager to get their hands on this rare book, but of course, because of the nature of its edition, most were disappointed. Only a lucky few managed to secure a copy for themselves. Ever since, we've steadily received requests for this collection, with many fans asking if a general release paperback would ever be available. Both Immanion Press and Tanith's husband, John Kaiine, feel that the time is now right for this expanded paperback edition.

Tanith Lee died over a year ago, on 24th May 2015. Several anthologies of her uncollected stories have been released since then, including Immanion Press's 'Legenda Maris'. This edition of 'Animate Objects', long-awaited by Tanith enthusiasts, makes these stories – some of them previously unpublished – available to all.

This book differs from the hardback collector's edition in two respects. The original illustrations of medieval gargoyles and other peculiar stone creatures have been replaced by a selection of pictures, by the artist Jarod Mills, commissioned especially for the book. Also, there are two new stories, co-written by Tanith and John Kaiine.

Now please sit back and enjoy this outstanding collection of Tanith's extraordinary tales. And remember, as Tanith will shortly tell you herself, you're quite safe – this book is an *inanimate* object… isn't it?

Introduction to the Original Edition

Tanith Lee

ear Reader

There is no such thing as an inanimate object.

Or do any of us truly believe there is?

Landscapes, of course, are alive. They grow and alter and shift. Grass rises tall, huge trees tower up from flimsy saplings. Earthquakes shake, landslides slip. Seas are usually tidal–and like the weather–have changes of mood. Deserts come–and go. And buildings–well, they turn into picturesque ruins; walls fall down. Or somehow go on miraculously standing for centuries. But machines, obviously Man makes machines. Just as he creates artwork and weapons.

Because it is the animal world, including the human animal, that moves and thinks and feels–for good or ill. It's we, *us*, that *gets things done.*

So what about that car then, that never wants to start for only *one* particular journey, yet always working fine otherwise, and with nothing anyone can find to be wrong with it? Or that corner that always stubs your toe, or that third step on the stair that nearly always trips you up. Who is one of those few who has *never* wanted to hurl their typewriter or computer through the window due to some crazy recurrent incompetence that really, and proveably, has nothing whatever to do with their use of it, let alone their skill?

Lifts and elevators (name immaterial) stick, vehicles stall, or take off on their own, phones and laptops go on the blink–or *mad*, it sometimes seems. Lights fuse just at the worst moment, oven-pressure drops for no reason and wrecks the dinner-party. *Why* does that picture keep falling off the wall? Why is it every time you wear that shirt something goes wrong–or *right*?

I have heard of, and experienced, endless varieties of such events. For example, the Sat-Nav that firmly insisted a friend of mine was driving through a river when she was safely negotiating a nicely-maintained thoroughfare. While I have been in a cab when the Sat-Nav, until switched off, sternly and repeatedly warned the driver we were in a field, when we were on the Brighton Road.

I'm an animist, though. I think everything–from the smallest pebble to the greatest mountain, the tiniest shot glass to a wall-to-wall TV, has a life-force in it. Ornaments do, toys do, buildings do. Walk into an empty room–you're not alone.

And how could that be? Because, simply, everything is formed from matter, and basically, at *root*, the matter that makes up everything in the physical world–the Universe–is of the same Playdoh substance. Out of this, however divergently–we–and *all* other things–evolve. Which means, on that basic level, (before we put on all our wonderful differences and disguises of bodies and shapes and *kinds*) we–you, me, and that Power Station over there–are all the exact riotous, chaotic, amorphous *same*.

For that reason the pebble and I, for me, are (very unlike) siblings. And if a Sat-Nav wants to lie to us, well, it makes a sort of sense why it might.

In the following collection is an assortment of Lee takes (so far) on the nature, and perhaps intentions, of so-called non-sentient things. Plus, inevitably, our relationships with them. But if you care to read the stories, don't worry. After all, this is only a book. An inanimate object. *Perfectly* safe.

Respectfully yours

Tanith Lee
September 2013

Arborium

Fires and walls,
        and wheels, and ships-
To warm us, shield us,
        make us free.
And then comes paper-
        parchment rips
Out scrolls, and books,
        and kills each tree.

Forgive my hand that writes
        your praises
Upon your *corpse.*
        In endless phrases.

The Occasional Table

nder the window... she can hear how something moves there softly, with a faint, continual scratching. Like the sound of old fallen leaves shuffled on concrete, only like that.

But the something isn't like that at all. And soon her companion will rejoin her, and then what–what in God's name–will she do?

Janet saw it in the window of the shop, just as she was giving up all idea of finding anything. Anything suitable, that was. She realised, of course, her view was subjective. It involved the wish to give a present to her sister that was desirable and would therefore be appreciated. But also it had to be a present Janet too could at least appreciate, if not desire. A thing that carried the stamp both of receiver and giver. In addition it must be affordable–yet not skimpy.

Her sister had good, if rather old-fashioned–or retro, was it?–taste. Plus the money, herself, to indulge it. Then there was her future husband to be considered.

Really, Leo hadn't ever seemed especially interested in any sort of ornament or furnishing, the very *type* of thing one gave prior to a marriage. Oh, such complications. There were others besides.

After all, if Marianne liked the bloody gift *naturally* so would he. (And irresistibly Janet recalled how Leo had changed his mobile phone to the exact model Marianne then currently used. How he had even decided to enjoy Mozart, as Marianne did, where two years ago he hadn't given a damn for anything but jazz).

Never mind all that.

Janet pushed open the shop door quite fiercely and went in among the junk/antiques.

These places seemed sad, even dejected to her. Objects people had loved and had to lose, through financial difficulties, or death, left here at the mercy of the casual and the hard-to-please.

But bending nearer to it now, Janet could see the little table was flawless; in fact beautiful. Although it looked rather dry. It should be polished.

She had sometimes noticed through the window an old man ambling about in here amid his merchandise, and was startled when a youngish, female person sprang out on her around a bookcase.

"*Yes?*" she screeched. In one hand she flourished a Spanish fan (for sale, its label said so). In the other was a sheaf of papers which now at once, to *show* Janet what a nuisance customers in a shop were, she dropped. "Oh *shit!*"

Janet, seeming pale and composed and perhaps disapp-roving, waited. Actually she was only rather afraid of people, and this hennaed harpy, at least a decade her junior, represented the manifestation of the Critical Adult–with which archetypal menace she had had knowingly to deal since her tenth year.

"Excuse me. The little table–that one over there?"

"It's not for sale."

"Yes it is. It says so."

"Speaks then, does it?" rudely snapped the red-head. Then, "You mean that one." She pointed accusingly. Janet followed the direction of the over-long, squared-off, outlandish fingernail.

"Yes."

"Thought you meant the dining-table. *That* is the occasional table. I said to *him*, *what* does *that* mean, for Christ's sake? And apparently it means it's a table for *infrequent* and *occasional* use. He even showed me in the dictionary. Typical."

"Really," said Janet, hoping soon to go very far away.

"It's Victorian. Or was it Georgian? Or 1920's?"

"I don't know. What are you asking for it?"

"*I'm* not asking for anything. Except a quiet life and fat chance of *that*. Where's his book? Oh right. Seventy pounds." Janet partly opened her mouth and the woman stridently added, "I can't haggle. He told me. It's seventy or nothing. Or you can speak to *him*. *He* isn't back until July."

It was early June, and the wedding was in thirteen days.

Janet wished she had found something at least twenty pounds less. But she had left the unwanted gift-shopping too late, and already been out all morning and afternoon, taking the train to the better shops, coming back here, walking and looking and walking and asking and walking. She wanted to conclude her false search for a lovely present for someone who, frankly, she hated. She wanted to get home and make strong tea, and then a stiff gin and tonic, and be done with this forever.

"We don't take credit cards. Look, it says on the wall," pontificated Henna.

"That's all right. I didn't think you would."

Luckily, a pessimist as life had taught her to be, Janet had come prepared.

That evening she polished the table with a proper beeswax, and dusters bought at the Emporium on the corner.

She repeated the procedure again three days before she was due to deliver the gift to Marianne and Leo's so-far empty new flat at Landseer Gardens. Here, as Janet saw, most of the other gifts had already arrived. (Some of the items Janet glimpsed there made her stare with a kind of dull fury. The flat too, which was located in a prestigious block overlooking a railed-off green park, and had several large rooms, and one enormous sitting room that Marianne, pretentiously Janet thought, had named the Parlour).

The polishing however had been pleasant, and somehow satisfying. The table too had seemed to enjoy it, burnishing up with a deep, almost golden inner glow. It was made of walnut, so its label said. Janet had read somewhere that walnut, and certain other trees employed for furniture, were beaten when growing. The scars this violence produced would later, when the tree was felled, provide wonderful inclusions and grain in the finished articles. She thought absently it was a terrible way to produce beauty–through cruelty. Like beating a helpless slave before killing her, in order to create interesting avante-garde patterns on the corpse.

But to polish the table now, bring up its grain, was also part of Janet's act of imprinting, of self-assertion. She had bought the costly table, and made it fair, so that Marianne–well-off, glamorous Marianne–could not despise it. So that Marianne would have to take a momentary interval from the obvious contempt in which she must, and did, hold her sister, Janet, if only whenever the table caught her eye. Which would be, of course, occasionally.

The wedding. Oh God, the wedding.

Two beautiful people, Marianne with her dark red (natural) hair, copper kettles transformed to silk. And he. Leo. Dark as night.

Oh God. The wedding.

A simple, non-religious ceremony.

A pleasant meal in a trendy restaurant.

Wonderful.

Two years ago, when Marianne was thirty, and Janet

thirty-nine, Janet and Leo had been lovers.

But that was then. This was–hell.

It was *hell.*

All her life Janet had felt inadequate. And then found out she *was.* Inadequate. *Redundant.*

Three months into their relationship, she and Leo had met Marianne and her 'then-man' for dinner. And, that was it.

Marianne's then-man was sloughed. Over the course of the next four months, Janet and Leo were drawn apart. As if a magnet pulled him (albeit willingly) away from her. At last they were quite separated.

Janet had continued with her own arid life, teaching, lecturing, travelling, sometimes in the way of her work She came back from a gruesome exchange stint in France one spring, and discovered Marianne and Leo were in love. They were living together. They were considering marriage.

By then Janet was almost forty-two. She was, she felt, unable ever to form a permanent liaison. And, although she had never burningly wished for children, any chance she might have had of conceiving and bearing a child by a man she loved, was gone.

Marianne, however.

Marianne: young enough, beautiful and strong enough, Marianne with her high-powered job on the fringe of fashion, Marianne in her *ultra* fashionable, eye-catching wedding wear black with silver–Marianne was just at the most perfectly ripened stage.

And Leo gazed at her from his symphony of darkness. Glorious black Leo, with his skin of shadow and real-university accent, and his heart like–like what? Like over-warmed wax.

When she came home from the wedding feast Janet, who had been so pale and calm and self-controlled, lay on her bed and noisily wept all night. The non-feather pillows filled with tears. A cliché. But, as often they are, true.

Apparently neither of them, such busy people and in such demand, had any time for a holiday then, and a week after their marriage Marrianne and her husband moved into their vast new flat.

Able always to hire help to assist them, the place had been readied, painted, dressed, and stocked with food and drink and all necessities, including several gigantic plants.

Four days more and they threw a flat-warming party, to which Janet, along with many other, (more important), guests was invited. Marianne informed her of this over the phone.

Janet attempted to get out of the date.

Marianne wouldn't hear of it.

"I won't hear of it, Jan. Come on, it'll be fun. Sometimes I think you can't stand us, the way you avoid us all the time." Playful, that. Cat with mouse? Janet was never sure. She never was sure with most people most of the time, whether they got at and insulted her from spite or only insensitivity. "And anyway, you *must* see where I put your table in the Parlour."

"My... oh, you mean the occasional table."

"What else. I'm sorry I didn't thank you properly," (she had not thanked Janet at all), "and I meant to write–but you know how it is. But you can see when you come over. It's a very nice piece, not quite like the rest of our stuff–but well, who cares–it's charming. And isn't it such a quaint breed? An *occasional* table. Now I wonder what that means–or did you make it up, Jan, as a joke?"

"No. It means–"

Marianne swam effortlessly on over Janet's voice "–I wondered if you meant it's only a table *occasionally*. That it can change into something else? I can't think what. A small chair perhaps, or a desk. Or do you think it's something animate? An osprey maybe–" Janet could hear Leo laughing at this wit in the background. How well Janet knew that laugh, deep, musical. How well she knew all of Leo. But never well enough, it seemed.

"Sorry, Marianne–my mobile's going. Have to answer it."

"OK, Jan. But I warn you, if you don't come to our party I shall drive over and drag you here."

Janet doubted this very much. Yet, as always it seemed to her she had to be, Janet knew she would be malleable, do as she was told, keep up the pretence of sisterliness, and go.

She only stayed two hours, pleading a six a.m. start for Leeds the following morning, although in reality she didn't have to set out until twelve. But the two hours were bad enough. Stood there in her best frock, with everyone else so sloppily and so expensively clad, and with the odd diamond or ruby in evidence, as in the engagement bracelet Leo had bought Marianne. It was funny really. When he had known Janet he had earned as little as she did. Perhaps she had held him back. Conversely, Marianne must have inspired him.

They, the two hosts, did seem to enjoy the evening.

He in black, she in scarlet, as if to match themselves, laughing, wrapping round each other–evidently they truly could not help it, even now electrically attracted–and the little whispers, the tiny in-jokes only they could understand.

"Aren't they just *sweet*?" remarked one of the designer-clad women to Janet. She seemed to have no axe to grind, to be genuinely delighted that Leo and Mar, as she called them, were this compatible. "They remind me of my kids–teenagers in love. But I suppose, when you're in love, it's always like that."

"Yes," lied Janet, and had another glass of the Bollinger.

Had it ever been like that, for her? She thought it hadn't. But probably all her loves had only ever been one-sided. *Her* love, not theirs. Her *lust* too, not theirs. She the convenience, something to use until the improved or suitable thing turned up.

She did see the table. It stood under the amber spotlight of one of the lamps, with a single miniature white porcelain box upon it.

She did not speak to the table, despite having spoken to it when she polished it. Stupid old cow, embarrassing enough to start talking to various objects when at home. Mustn't start to do it when in public.

But she stared at the table, and touched its surface lightly with one finger. At least the help, Consuelo, would keep it dusted.

To her great surprise Janet didn't cry that night at all. She fell into the bed and slept right through until the alarm went off at eight o'clock.

Doubtless all that Bollinger.

"Do you think she really *tries* to avoid us, Leo?"

"Yeah. But–I don't *know*," he said.

"I pummel my brains. I don't see if I just leave her alone–or keep on trying to keep contact. She–she isn't easy, but Jan means a lot to me, you know. When I was a kid and Dad–they say women nag, but *he*–well she sort of used to head him off. And when I got depressed she used to tell me I was pretty."

"She was wrong."

"*Thank* you"'

"Not pretty. You're sensational."

"Better. But can you even *imagine* Janet using a word like that? She's so..."

"Closed." He sighed. "Shut, bolted and barred. I never knew what went on in her head. You're like an open book–"

"Gee, thanks."

"A *wonderful* open book. Unputdownable. And you can read me pretty well–"

"Better believe it, babes."

"She never seemed to know when I needed her–or when to leave me alone. Or didn't she care if she knew? I thought she was all wrapped up in her work. That came first. Selfish. But she isn't because–well, because."

"You and me."

"She couldn't have been more–"

"Understanding?"

"More–*tactful*. But then if I never meant that much–"

"You know you don't think that. And I–I thought she loved you. I felt bloody guilty sometimes, you know."

"If that was her loving me–she never showed it to me. I mean, apart from the obvious, and even there, when we had sex–not cold, but cool... tepid. That sounds–I'm not trying to bad-mouth or denigrate. Only–I never even knew if she liked it, with me."

A murmur beside him, "With me, however–"

There in the soft, custom-built, 3a.m. bed, the lovers, amalgamated, mouth to mouth, and suddenly outside a strange short thud, and then the bright splash of something small, shattering.

"*Christ–*"

"Leo–*don't* go out–someone must have broken in–"

"They can't, not without the alarm goes off. Fucking hell–"

He leapt from the bed.

The bedroom door undone and flung wide.

Along the corridor, the wide cave-opening of the huge room they call the Parlour. All in darkness, just the vague half-glims of streetlamps through thick blinds and part-drawn silk curtains–

Now nothing stirs, nothing moves or makes a sound.

Leo pads through into the room, naked, clothed only in his strong fit body, and switches on the overhead light.

"Jesus."

He sounds upset, but not afraid or in danger. Marianne comes running along the corridor, also naked but for the Victorian male nightshirt she has thrown on.

"Oh! My Chinese box–"

It lay in a tiny static snowstorm of white bits. Just below the rounded wooden paws of the new table.

"Some bloody wanker must have picked the box up and put it back too near the edge. Maybe a truck went by, the vibration."

"We don't ever get that in here. And nothing at all went by, we'd have heard that, too."

"Well then someone moved it, Dirk, bet it was him. Look, the table isn't where it was either, is it."

"No... it's right over there by the side window–I never noticed when we went to bed. I didn't really look."

Even in partial light the room now seemed rather a sordid mess, littered with used glasses and plates, the empty bottles adrift in melted ice, the wilting salad leaves.

Consuelo would clear up in the morning. She would clear the broken box too, put the table back in place under the lamp.

He said, "Come on. It's dawn in about two minutes."

July filled the city, turned the sky to hard blue slate. A heatwave began, attributed instantly to global warming, as (Janet thought) every sunny month, heavy rain, winter snow-flurry or high wind now was.

She had got back from Leeds anxious and sore-throated from giving three lectures, (always inevitably impaired by her stage fright), and exhausted too from being so much with strangers.

The ansaphone had several routine business messages, and one from her sister.

"Jan? I think you're back tomorrow–or is it Monday? Can you give me a call when you do? Nothing serious just, well, just something I'd like to ask you. Sort of really *need* to know. Bye."

Janet, to her slight astonishment, shuddered from head to toe, as if from an abrupt drop in temperature, or some other thing far worse. Despite her feelings, she had never in her life before experienced such an extreme reaction to Marianne's mere voice.

What did she want? No doubt a stupid, aggravating thing. An unnecessary reassurance. A favour Janet must perform. If it was another invitation, Janet would have her excuses marshalled in readiness.

She meant to put it off, but the message bugged her. Marianne sounded rather odd. What could she possibly think Janet might know that she, the marvellous Marianne, was ignorant of?

"Marianne?"

"Oh hi! Hi, Jan. Have a good trip? Bet you wowed 'em. Look, just wanted to ask you something."

"So you said in your message."

"Well, it'll sound bats, but here goes. That table you bought us."

The table. The table again.

"What about it?" *Does she want to know what I paid for it? Want to sell it on at a profit–*

"Do you remember the shop you got it from?"

"Yes."

"Well, look, Jan... did they say anything about it? I mean like where it came from? Who'd sold it– why– Anything?"

"No. Why would they?"

"Shit. Hoped they had. You weren't curious?"

Janet thought, *No. Am I now?*

She said quietly, "If you don't like it, Marianne, if it doesn't go with your stuff–"

"Well it doesn't, quite, but I did *like* it. Leo thought it was OK too. Do you remember how we had it?"

"Yes."

"Under the big lamp, with the little box on top."

"Yes."

Janet heard her sister draw in a long breath. Marianne said, "It's a bit busy. You know."

"What do you mean?"

"Well it–you're not going to– It moves about, Janet. It moves about by itself. It's never in the place we put it. It usually goes–yes, I know this sounds wildly insane–it seems to like to go over to a window. Leo says it likes to look out, but that's Leo being Leo. You know, like he is."

I don't know, Janet thought. She replied flatly, "You're saying the table walks round your room to the windows and then watches the street."

"Oh don't put it like that, Jan. Of course it can't watch or walk. Only it does move–I mean *we* don't move it–except to put the bloody thing back where we had it. And Consuelo swears she only dusts it, and anyhow it happens when she isn't here. It happens mainly at night. Or, just yesterday evening–I was here with Annie–you know Annie from *New Age Angel*? Anyway, we were in the kitchen making strawberry soup and there was a crash, and we ran into the Parlour and all Annie's stuff, and her lap-top too, off the couch and on the floor, and the table, well the table sort of standing there on the proofs she'd brought to show me. Yes. Sort of standing there on them."

"Marianne–"

"I'm not going certifiable, Jan." Marianne giggled winningly. "Leo's had run-ins with it as well. He says it's haunted or *possessed*. But I say it's some kind of poltergeist or something–or what do they call it? Telly Kineese?"

"Telekinesis."

"Janet, I'm not lying. Cross my tits and hope to fly. Honestly. It just *moves*. I mean, I'm not *scared*. I'm *curious*. So I wondered–"

Janet said, feeling uncoil in herself a sudden unrecognised, or perhaps never-acknowledged, slow and metallic vein of pitilessness, "Marianne, sorry. My mobile's going. Have to call you back."

And cutting the connection, Janet unplugged her telephone.

So hot, that July. The hottest July, they said, in living memory. Which meant what? A hundred years?

But Marianne said to Leo, "Christ, the carbon footprint.

Let's switch off the air-conditioning."

And both of them, anyway, *liked* the heat. They had lain prone on enough beaches, she soaking up the sun to gold, he soaking to ebony. Why not then turn the wretched ozone- depleting machine off and open the windows like ordinary people and simply–*bask*?

They did it.

They sat on their balcony and fed each other cashew nuts and walnuts to celebrate, and drank Geneva with ice.

Then they went out, barefoot on pavements toasted as sunflower seeds, to dinner at the *Salamander*.

To be so happy, surely it wasn't a crime? They weren't hurting anyone, were they? They'd even switched off the air-conditioning.

Strolling back hand in hand around midnight, the slimline block of apartments came in view, and something was very different.

"What the fuck–?"

"They're fire engines, Leo! And two police vans–"

A sort of light official cordon was around the flats, men standing about. Leo spoke to a lazy-looking officer in charge.

"It's all right, sir. Don't think there's much to worry about. Some woman saw something climbing up the building, she says."

"Something?"

"A big cat, she thought. Or a monkey. Escaped from the zoo, she thought, sir." The policeman smiled slightly.

"It's OK for us to go in?"

"Absolutely fine, sir. We're just finishing up here."

There was an RSPCA van at the kerb too; an enraged man stood beside it, talking incomprehensibly on a mobile.

They went into the foyer, where the porter nodded, "Right to-do."

"What happened?"

"A lady on the floor below your own. She and her friend

saw something on the outside wall. Probably a disturbed pigeon."

"The guy in charge said she thought it was a big cat–some kind of puma? Panther?"

"Yes. Well. Perhaps she was a bit... tired. But nowadays, all this terrorism... don't want to take chances."

When they got upstairs and turned the lights on everything looked undisturbed, and outside the cordon had broken up and official van after van was driving away.

They were about to take a shower together when the telephone rang.

"Leave it, Marianne. Who calls this late?"

"Just–in case. Hello?"

An unknown female agitated voice filled her ear. "My name is Stephanie Avery, I live on the floor below. I hope you won't mind, I got your number from the inquiry service. I'm sorry about all the fuss with police and so on. But I *did* see something. Lucy did too. We both did. It went past my window."

"You saw an animal climbing the building." Marianne sounded very patient.

"Yes. Yes, we did. We both did. I don't know what it was. Less climbing up than round and up and down. It was very sinuous, almost like a snake, Lucy said. But with arms–legs–I don't know. I've been in Africa, you see. I'm used to animals clambering all over the house. But not here. Not *here*."

"Well, maybe try to get some sleep."

"*Sleep*. I don't think I'll sleep tonight."

Leo and Marianne went into the shower, washed among the waters and had sex. Only when they finally got to bed around two-thirty did Marianne realise the table, for once, had been exactly where they had left it. Deeply asleep about an hour later, she dreamed something with long claws was scratching at their shut bedroom door. It was the cat wanting to come in, only they didn't have a cat. She didn't like cats, and Leo had little interest in animals. But even so the cat kept on and on. And also, though asleep, with a sort of shame Marianne recalled they had left the air-conditioning going in this one area, their bedroom. Only a *tiny* carbon footprint, like that of a baby, or the pawprint of a cat. But they mustn't. They really must not, unless the temperature went way over a hundred. Tomorrow, turn it off. *Scratch* said the door in the dream, and the cat at the door in the dream.

Janet dreamed she was running over heathland, low and hillocky, in darkness without a moon. In her right hand she carried a Spanish fan with a tag on it that declared it was for sale, but in her left hand she bore a spear. She had never knowingly held a spear before, and was not left-handed, but in the dream the stance and action seemed familiar and appropriate, indeed useful.

She had been hunting something, or so she felt when she woke up. A hunter's dream. Except, asleep, she never caught it.

Of course neither of them had been frightened by the antics of the table. (*Antics* had been a favourite word of Marianne and Janet's mother; somehow it seemed the most suitable one now).

Leo, who claimed the table was possessed, had firstly studied it, trying to catch it out. But it was always the case that they never *saw* it move, only, later, that it must have done. It was mostly nocturnal. Or had been. The episode with Annie's lap-top was startlingly repeated the morning after their dinner at *Salamander* and the police presence outside the flats, when Marianne and Leo were woken by a colossal crash from the main region of the flat.

This time the event had not taken place in the Parlour. The kitchen provided an arena, where a stack of dirty bone-china plates and mugs were lined up, because Consuelo was on holiday for the next six days, and they had cancelled the agency girl. Every plate and mug had been swept off on to the tiled floor, and was subsequently in smithereens.

Marianne wailed. She had liked the plates.

Leo said sternly, "Stop it, Mar. You sound like my Aunt Ginger."

And Marianne, turning to remind him she was not eighteen stone and three-quarters cracked, never spoke because that was when she saw the table. The occasional table.

It was standing (after all, you could say a table 'stood', couldn't you) in the little annexe where they had put the washing machine. As an animal might that has just stolen food from a counter or out of the fridge, not exactly cowering, afraid of your reaction, certainly not guilty, but–wary, watchful. Ready to defend, perhaps to attack?

Marianne's spine went icy cold, even in the loud bronze heat of un-air-conditioned 11.30 a.m. This was because she thought, finally, she *had* seen the table move.

It was a sort of flexing–like that, or even like the shiver that passes over a briefly disturbed pool. A *dark* shiver–sinuous, as the old woman downstairs had said–*snakelike*–

"Leo– I–"

"What?" He glared at her impatiently.

Normally when he got this way she let him be. But now she wasn't going to. "Leo I don't want it in our flat anymore."

"Don't want what?"

"For Christ's sake, Leo, who–*what*–do you think did this?"

"OK," he said. "The table. Right." He looked bewildered, then a little shaken. "When I go out I'll dump it by those bins in Crap Street–" This was their name for the rundown mews that lay the other side of the gardens.

"Yes, Leo. I'd–like that."

"What'll you say if Janet comes round and wants to know

where it is?"

"*Fuck* Janet," Marianne flared.

And Leo turned away because, obviously, a couple of years ago and quite regularly, he had done that very thing.

Below, in her own flat, old Stephanie Avery, who was actually only fifty-four, was talking it through all over again with Lucy, on the phone. To start with, Stephanie had confessed to feeling slightly embarrassed she had called the people upstairs. She must have sounded potty. And for another thing they had annoyed her for weeks with noise–who would ever have imagined Mozart could be played at such volume? Sometimes there were other sounds. But the loudest of these were at least human (animal), and never lasted long.

Soon though the conversation with Lucy shifted back to the creature on the wall.

"You know," said Lucy, "the thing I think it really reminded me of the most was a giant spider."

Stephanie frowned. "There weren't enough legs." Even when rattled she was a realist, a fact she had learned about herself when in Africa. "And no spider could be as large as that."

"Oh, I know. It was simply–something about it. The way it moved. And the other thing, although perhaps you *did* notice them–only I couldn't see that it had any eyes."

"No, that's true. Surely they must have gleamed at some point, catching our light or the streetlamps–the way it was turning round, round and round, and going up and then down–as if..." Stephanie paused.

Lucy concluded the sentence, "–it was searching for something?"

"But what?"

"A way," said Lucy, "in?"

By the time they rang off, Stephanie's black neighbour Leo, eccentrically carrying a small table tucked into his arm, was walking along the pavement below. Stephanie saw him from her window and, with a slight discomfort, strode briskly across the room to turn up her own air-conditioning. Global warming did not particularly trouble her, and the idea of switching off the coolness and opening the window did not appeal, not at all.

When he dumps the table in the alley with the bins, Leo finds he is glad to put it down. He brushes off his arm, which has a vague prickly feel to it, as if he has had contact with a milder type of nettle.

But that's only the superstitious side to him that he has worked so hard to eradicate. Aunt Ginger would have insisted on a full Catholic exorcism for the table. Or another kind of service maybe, with beads and bones and a cut-throated chicken–

Before he walks away to catch the eco-conscious bus, he glances back at the table.

It stands exactly where he set it, next to the most malodorous and least recycled dustbin. It is entirely still. And–almost surreal, so dainty, so polished, left all alone in squalor. Someone will come by and grab it, he thinks. Sell it, probably.

Frankly, they could tell Janet just that, if it came to it–that some dinner guest had fancied and pinched it, draping it with his coat. This is, if she ever shows up in their lives once more. Which somehow he doubts Janet ever will. But then, he wouldn't miss her if he never saw her again.

All that day Janet had a strong urge to call Marianne. But to say or suggest what?

Janet didn't want to meet her sister. Didn't even want to talk to her on the telephone.

So what was it?

About ten times now she had gone over to the phone, put her hand on it. Once she had taken her mobile out of her bag, started to press the numbers for Marianne's landline. Ridiculous. She turned her mobile off.

Janet had a new talk to write, partly learn, and simplify into matching prompt notes. She never gave a talk without this preliminary care, not since the time she had completely dried, on a platform in Manchester, before an audience of four hundred people.

But she couldn't concentrate on the material, and about 5p.m.she left it and poured herself a small gin.

"What am I going to do with my life?"she asked the old word processor she still preferred to utilise. "Or even with the bloody evening?"

She sat down and peered at the local newspaper, last refuge of the desperate.

But this was it, after all. She, who gave talks, had no one to talk *to* but the furniture and fittings of her drab studio flat, and only a radio and TV to talk to *her*. You couldn't keep pets here, not in this crumbling 'renovated' house, not that she had ever wanted a pet. She had wanted– Oh Christ, she had wanted Leo. That was all. And now, still that was all.

She sat there and told the dregs of the small gin and tonic that tomorrow she would go to see a movie, alone of course, but even so. And then have supper somewhere, alone of course but even so.

But even so.

Since much of the district had been named after the artist Landseer, (Landseer Terrace, Landseer Road East, Landseer Gardens), an assortment of the newspapers that presently carried reports, coined for the phenomenon the term *The Landseer Lynx*.

These were only short paragraphs, however.

Someone on the radio the next day alluded to the 'Lynx' nevertheless. He remarked that as at least ten people, (all of whom either informed the police or the RSPCA), claimed to have seen the animal, it was perhaps less likely to be a hoax than a form of mass hallucination.

Only a single paper meanwhile mentioned that there had been a previous sighting.

It seemed the 'Lynx' was either black in colour, or a very dark brown. It had, some of the witnesses said, a very shiny or sheeny coat. There had been something incongruous about the head, and apparently no one had been able to be sure it had a tail–a couple feared it had lost the tail in an accident. But it moved very fast–in a sort of "jerky glide" as one young woman put it. The reported places of its swift emergences and equally swift exits from view, ranged from the corner of Landseer Terrace, outside *The Stag* pub in Landseer Road East, up which and out of which it 'darted', 'ran' or 'jerkily glided' into Landseer Crescent, and the small private park at Landseer Gardens. There had also been one other sighting. This by a homeless person intending to visit some dustbins in Cropton Mews. But as he did not tell anyone about the thing he saw, nor the wave of feral horror and panic that had overcome him and caused him to take to his heels in the opposite direction, his evidence was never added to the hallucinatory list.

Marianne woke up from a deep sleep in which she had been having a peculiar and unenjoyable dream. She lay motionless, trying to recollect what it had been about. But the dream was entirely gone, or very nearly, for its miasmic quality still hung low in her brain. Think of something else.

After a moment she looked at the luminous face of her clock: 2 a.m.

The night was hot and cindery-smelling, the summer city smell that for her, always, spelled both excitement and normalcy.

Beside her Leo stretched, silently and completely sleeping. How gorgeous he was. In a moment she'd turn and burrow into his back. Then he might himself wake up, and they would make lovely, lovely love again.

She felt much better, but wide awake.

It was very quiet outside, one of those nights when, she thought, there was no sound at all. Of course there *was* though, when you examined it. Additionally, virtuous greens that they were, the bedroom air-conditioning was now off and the window open wide, full of the 1ight-poluted milky electric city-night sky, and any noise amplified–or rather, evident through its unshielded state.

Yes, now she could hear traffic endlessly in motion along Landseer Road East, a long, dull gush like a river... and far off laughter, thin and shrill. And she could hear the crossing beeping on one of the other roads, and a plane droning above the overcast, and maybe *that* was distant thunder?–it was hot enough for a storm–and a little scrape-scrape sound, like something brushing along the wall–

What could that be? Marianne asked herself, uninterestedly. She could feel sleep washing back after all. Just turn a bit, and lie against Leo, and shut her eyes...

The scraping thing outside was louder. Perhaps it was actually down on the street, something blowing along... only there wasn't any wind, not even a breeze–odd. Yes, definitely more loud than before. A sort of sharpness to it now. Something quite hard, scraping up the brickwork–

Marianne opens her eyes and glances, with what she knows to be an infantile apprehension, at the big unguarded space of the window. Her timing is exquisite. For it is exactly then that the thing which has scraped its way up the wall enters the opening and begins to unfurl itself, leg by leg, down into the room.

Four days after when, alerted by a sickening stink, the porter was summoned and went into the opulent flat above, discovering there two most abnormally dead bodies, (he would never get over it), Stephanie Avery had to confess she had heard them, both of them, screaming, on what must have been the night of their murder. She was naturally incredibly shaken. She explained, red in the face with distress, that she had just assumed they were watching 'some film'. "They did, you see, make quite a lot of noise. They played music till all hours, classical music–but ridiculously loudly. It's the modern type of instruments. I've heard musicians go deaf now in symphony orchestras–and I'm not at all surprised they do. And they had DVD's, very noisy–gunshots and uproar. I thought it must be just another of those. I'd kept meaning to speak to them about it, the noise, I mean. But you know the way people are now. I didn't want to make enemies. So–oh God, these past few days I'm afraid I was just so glad they were being quiet for a change–"

Despite the physical decomposition due to time and the heat, the police surgeon had been baffled by the bodies. And having performed a post mortem, not the easiest task given their condition, he remained baffled.

His report limited itself to facts. But a month later he confided to an old friend that he had never seen anything of the sort in his life. Hoped, if he were honest, never to see anything like it ever again. "The state of the organs could–*just*–have been due to the weather, though I've come across bodies left longer in hotter climes, and they weren't in such a mess. But the eyes, not that. Nor the blood or bones. You probably won't believe me, Henry," (Henry assured him that he would), "there was no marrow. Absolutely none. Something had somehow–got it out. Sucked them dry. And the bones, what was left of them–were broken, every one.

Even the skulls had given way. Not as if from any violent blow–but as if–what can I say–I don't know what I can say. As if they had *melted.* Inspector Warden was on it, he was thinking of manic burglars with acids and suction pumps, you know what he's like." (Henry said he did). "But no human, or mechanised–not even any animal agency I can think of–could be responsible. And nobody had any lead. DNA? Forget it. The case has been hushed up, obviously. Sometimes, such awful things must happen. No explanation, no excuse. No solution. They interviewed a sister of the dead girl. Warden said she might have had a reason to cause harm. I forget what it was. But she couldn't have done this. No one–no one and nothing I ever heard of–*could*."

But something had.

That night, the very night the Landseer Lynx roamed and glided with its odd jerky grace and headless, tailless, four-legged running–

Although it was a shape-shifter, it was still a solid and animate thing, and only small. It had therefore been quite unable to breach the bathroom or bedroom doors, which Marianne and Leo, both curiously prudish, always kept closed when in use or at night, (the shape-shifter's most urgent time), because they liked sex in the shower or the bed.

And bed or shower too were the only times when they were naked, the more easily to wash or to obtain each other. Even on the two occasions when it had drawn them both from cover, Marianne had prissily pulled on her man's nightshirt.

It had a difficulty, it seems, even with clothes. It had needed its prey to be unpeeled. Ready. Waiting.

But then they undid the windows. And out it climbed, and going around and around, and up and down the building, it tried to locate in its infallible, blind-seeing way, their window. But *their* window (the bedroom) that time, was shut.

It did not know to thank the spectre of carbon footprints for that final hot darkness, when it was already free and on the streets, and *every* window of the flat stood invitingly wide. And every stitch of clothing and sheet were off. And there they lay, black and white, and firm and luscious, on their bed of love. All ready for its thirsty un-mouth and its hungry lonely greedy heart.

Under the window... she can hear how something moves there softly, with a faint, continual scratching. Like the sound of old fallen leaves shuffled on concrete, only like that.

But the something isn't like that at all. And soon her companion will rejoin her, and then what–what in God's name–will she do?

Janet had been dreaming. It had made her feel alarmed, and somehow exhilarated. But she couldn't remember the dream's substance.

Tomorrow, although she doesn't know this quite yet, the police are going to knock on her door. She is going to turn white with genuine shock–not the shock of terror or grief, of course, the shock of the enormity of what has been accomplished. Yet no blame will adhere to her. That's undeniable.

Tonight however, on the brink of revelation, she is only slightly irritated by that scratching noise outside her open summer night window. It must be a rat, she thinks, down in the debris that always accumulates in the so-called garden.

Which is why, when the something becomes louder and much closer, she sits up in bed in dismay, then rises and walks to the window to shut it fast–

Except that in this exact moment, the creature about to be dubbed *The Landseer Lynx*, the shape-shifter, flows in and springs down on to the floor.

In this alter-form it is amazingly fluid, and its skin, if that *is* a skin, is less like a lynx pelt than the covering of a young shark seen in water. It gleams, like polished wood.

As well it might. Only on one side, the curve of side that faces her, are five little bumpy excrescences, like scars perhaps, knots in the wood of a tree caused by some sort of willful damage. These, though they have no look of that to them at all may, possibly, approximate a pair of ears, two (lightless) eyes, and a tiny mouth-area, toothless, tongueless, yet–for now–the merest fraction open. Then it closes the mouth, which it seems effortlessly able to do, just as so fluidly it moves its four unjointed yet plasticinely-agile legs.

Janet stares. She sees, (blindly, rather as it does), the small balls of feet like paws, with their slight impression of talons, which appear to have become a little stained. But the mouth is the worst. Even in the skewed glow of streetlamps from the road, she can tell at once it is slavered with something jellyish and bloody. (She thinks of a child who has been out playing and got muddy.)

"I'll have to tidy you up, wipe you clean," she says, absently. "And then polish you. That should be enough."

And then the creature comes to her and leans against her leg, and she touches the flat top of it with one finger, and with a quiver of pleasure it shifts. And stills. And is once again, the occasional table.

Fornian
Pinot Blonde
12 X 750 ML

Torhec the Sculptor

Beauty must die.....

–*The Beast,* Eric Sarusande

It was the thirteenth month and Christmas this year fell on the 23rd of Endember. On Christmas evening Aamon took his favourite mistress, Jacinte, to dinner at his preferred restaurant.

Once they had been seated in the golden half-light–the restaurant maintained a deliberately rustic air–she began to notice how alert and excited he seemed. Was it something he was dying to tell her, or something he was determined to keep to himself?

"You look very tired, Aamon," she therefore perversely said, sipping the champagne. "It's always so nice to see you, but please, never put my pleasures before your own good health."

Aamon smiled, and ate an olive and a chestnut. He said, "In fact I'm not tired at all. I am wildly elated."

"Mmm?" she asked with an indulgent smile.

"I shan't tell you in here. Wait until we have our coffee on the private terrace."

Aamon van Glanz was a multinaire. He was worth, so far

as she knew, uncountable amounts of wealth, mountains of which floated, in several staunch currencies, inside the ghostly spaces of the financial web. Additionally, he was quite good-looking, and a tolerable lover. She had been delighted when, three years before, he met her at a theatre party in the Old District, and began to show an interest. He never took up too much of her life; he usually retained five or six women at a time. His gifts to her were excellent, and occasionally savagely expensive.

They ate their leisurely meal, talking of other things. At about 11:30, going out to the private terrace, with its pleasant divans, coffee, liqueurs, chocolates, and a (quite fake) utterly convincing view of the heavens free of all interference, and alight with slowly wheeling planets and cascades of brilliant rhodium stars, he shut the door and locked it and said to her, "My love, have you ever seen any of the work of the sculptor Torhec?"

Jacinte had not. She had this in common with a great many billion people. Although, in the "civilised" world, most people had *heard* of his work, and certainly knew his name.

"Torhec, of course. But I've never been to one of his exhibitions."

"I'd have thought you might. If not for the preliminary art, for the subsequent violence, at least."

Jacinte looked deliberately vague. Here and there she had experienced–as now–a strange impression Aamon might be getting at her in some obscure, self-amusing, unusually clever way. Which was probably absurd.

"Well," he filled in, "I have. I have been to the very latest show of his, at the Gloewar Gallery. In all I went twice. Once at the opening in November, and again last month, when it ended."

"Was it good?"

"Oh, yes, beloved. Very *very* good. It was superb."

"Which part did you prefer? The sculptures–or... the

destruction?"

"In an odd way, both. I rather respect what he seems to have said. I can see the point of it.

"But surely," she murmured, "if everyone behaved as Torhec does, or is said to–nothing would be left."

"But that *is* his point. Nothing *is* left, ever, or ultimately can be."

Jacinte pulled an involuntary face and quickly pulled it back to charming creamy sweetness. "Suppose Leonardo da Vinci had thought the same," she added teasingly, wistfully, "or all of the great geniuses. No Leonardos then, no Michaelangelos. No Picassos or Kentys or Marlettes–"

"But in the end, the *end,* dear Jassy, those artworks too will be gone. They'll finally rot or crumble, or in the case of Marlette's glass–break. Or, if all else fails to spoil them, they'll melt or fry when the earth at last drops into the sun–or freeze and shatter when the sun goes out–whichever theory one subscribes to. Even the photographs or movies or holograms made of them will be lost." He gestured expansively to the recreation of space beyond the terrace. "Even that wonderful vista out there, and I don't mean just a replica, will one day dissolve into non-being. It *all* gets lost. Even us, or what's left of us. Nothing, ultimately, can remain of *anything.* That is precisely Torhec's point."

Jacinte raised her glass of wine, and stared into the tiny distortion of her mirrored beauty. *And I too? One day I will be old, one day I'll be dead. I must,* thought Jacinte with optimistic revival, *get someone really good–and sane–to paint me, and film* **me**, *as soon as I can.*

When she surfaced from this reverie, she grasped quite some time had elapsed. Aamon now seemed only ordinary. His excitement had either been dissipated, or suppressed, and she felt a sharp twist of curiosity after all. He had been going to tell her something? Or only this news of seeing an exhibition, followed by his little lecture on the nature of decay and transience. Reluctantly, at last she said, "But what was the secret you were going to reveal to me, Aamon?"

He seemed bemused. 'Was I? I wonder what I meant? There's nothing, Jassy... Unless, perhaps, this," he concluded, placing before her the gift box in which lay a flawless diamond choker.

To return to his second visit to the Gloewar, multi-rich Aamon had easily acquired a ticket. And though there were always crowds, both at the opening and the close of a Torhec exhibition, Aamon was positioned on a plush chair in the front row, accompanied only by his bodyguard, Brack. Like everyone else they were then issued with goggles; others had requested and received full-face, head- and/or body-shields. Twice, before such precautions had been put in place, people in the audience were wounded at the climax of the show.

Torhec, however, had entered the room clad only in shirt and pants, the shirtsleeves rolled up almost to his shoulders to reveal the muscular arms of a dedicated sculptor. His feet, large yet shapely, were quite bare, and nothing protected his valuable eyes at all. That too was, perhaps, in keeping with his beliefs.

His eyes, this way readily visible, were large and of a deep brown. His hair, thick and very dark, was complemented by his long eyebrows, and the short, trimmed, dense moustache and beard, which inked in his jaw and uncompromising mouth. In build he was stocky and tall, evidently immensely strong, his skin brown and here and there lightly scarred, most noticeably on his right cheekbone. His hands, like his feet, were large but beautiful, his most handsome features other than his eyes.

Glancing once at the audience, he lifted his right hand in a polite and peaceful gesture that was also incredibly dismissive. It had one extra quality: it seemed to draw across the huge room, dividing himself and his creations from all else, a transparent wall of damage-proof glass. Naturally this was not to protect anyone. It was merely to distance and keep others out. Aamon had heard, in fact, that several times at early displays of this "closing ceremony"–as the media had lately come to call it–maddened enthusiasts had rushed forward, attempting to prevent the final act. Gallery police had stopped these interventions, but clearly Torhec had perfected an added precaution of psychic room-division. It was a sort of magic, and no doubt he placed his faith in it. Certainly that evening it worked. No one rose to object. Only a few cries rang out at the commencing carnage. Then there was total quiet, but for the blows and their results, and occasional involuntary human noises–a cough, a grunt–and afterwards, when all had been done, hearty applause. Aamon had not joined in either outcry or congratulation. He preserved, as did the seven-foot, stoical Brack, (and Torhec himself), utter silence throughout.

Behind the non-actual glass shutter, Torhec at first paused briefly. Various people claimed he did this in order to bid grim or fond farewell to the fruits of his talent. Torhec himself had never, in any interview or other communication, endorsed this theory.

Aamon marked the little lacuna. It took, he noted, less than fifteen seconds.

Then Torhec picked up the hammer from the bench.

In size it was substantial, made of sustainable oak, and steel. He hefted it without effort, strong as a bull, high above his raven head.

Originally the works had been ranged all across the room, and some too were displayed in an annex, where a fountain played. Prior to the "closing ceremony" each one had been carefully relocated to half of the room Torhec now occupied. Accordingly they presented a rather muddled crowd of items. (No one who had not previously visited the exhibition would, today, have been able to tell much about them. Approximately one third of the audience comprised just such people. They were only interested in the endgame.)

The statues and statuettes were of differing materials. Some were hewn from stone, some made of plaster; here and there rose a marble form, and there were two of wood. None stood taller than four feet. They were mostly human in type, of both genders, abstractly clothed or naked, but there were too a group of slender, plant-like creations twisted among their own branches, and a single obelisk in reddish burnished stone. Aamon, who *had* visited the exhibition previously, had then examined each of the pieces with great attention. He had seen each was abundant in the most exquisite detail. All were graceful to an almost supernatural degree, and beautiful, a few in curious, nearly sinister ways–critics had tried to explain them, unavoidably, perhaps successfully, or not. Aamon did not try to explain, even to himself. His victorious life had not been founded on explanations. No sketch, photograph, video, or hologram had ever been permitted of the works of Torhec. Only the fading mental pictures could not be prevented; memories. Inevitably, in the majority of cases, they would be faulty, as are, generally, even those of the grieved-for dead.

The hammer smashed home with its blast of demolition, and the initial brief flurry of oaths and shrieks from the audience. A blizzard of broken white and gray exploded up and scattered down. Once begun Torhec did not hesitate. Inside two minutes five of the smaller artworks had been reduced to rubble. These chunks, even the most shapeless ones, the sculptor continued to mash, until they were only crumbs, splinters, dust. He was immensely thorough. It was his policy to be so. All creatures, things, all beauty–perished, and so should this.

Soon the air was thick with whitish fog. Those who had not requested facemasks, or used other improvised protection, coughed in an intermittent strangled undertone.

Eventually only six figures were left. These were the forms carved from wood, the bigger marbles, and the red obelisk.

Torhec laid the hammer aside and took up the first of the group of flasks also ready on the bench. They contained special mixes of corrosive. As he poured them over the last of his work, the audience watched in wonder as wood and stone bubbled and smoked, curling over, melting, flowing down to unidentifiable puddles on the floor. Torhec finalised things with the hammer, bashing to dust any lingering element. (Later, cleaners would come to clear the wreckage, sweep away the smoky dirt and suck up the more glutinous remains. These too, where human, were strictly monitored. Machines watched and ultimately frisked them, since not even a fragment of powder might be saved (filched) from this Armageddon.)

At the close, the audience started applauding frenziedly. Aamon and Brack were the only persons who did not applaud.

Torhec took little or no notice of any response. He again confronted the chairs, offered them a curt bow. His face was expressionless. He turned briskly and strode out of the room.

When everyone repaired to the cleared annex with the fountain, where tables loaded with alcohol and delicacies attended on the guests, Brack approached one of the gallery's aides and presented Aamon's card for the attention of the management.

Aamon van Glanz met Torhec personally late in December.

The venue now was Aamon's exclusive club on Westnorth Boulevard. In a private coffee-room Aamon had waited–Torhec was rather late–and when the sculptor entered, the entire nut-brown and gilded-parlour seemed to shrink and drain of colour.

Torhec, that big man who carried himself, Aamon now saw, always with careless ease, sat down facing him.

I'm late," said Torhec. This statement was the only apology Aamon was to receive. Another then, perhaps, who did not build on explanations.

"So you are. Would you like coffee?"

"I'll take brandy, thank you."

Aamon, who had researched what was known of Torhec's preferences, passed him the bottle.

Torhec had shrugged off his winter coat. Underneath, he still wore only shirt and pants, albeit different ones. His feet at least had been ensconced in boots, his hands in heavy gloves before he stripped them.

"It'll be Christmas in less than a month," Aamon remarked. "Do you have plans?"

"Yes," said Torhec. He drank some brandy, thought about it, and swallowed the contents of the glass bulb. Aamon leant forward and refilled it. Torhec said, "And the reason for this meeting?"

"Aside from the pleasure of contacting one of our foremost artists?" Aamon smiled. "I'd like to commission you."

"Really? I suppose that can be arranged." Torhec seemed not particularly enthused. For two years the public had been clamouring for his skills, in the city, next everywhere in the whole country and beyond. "I'm working," Torhec said, not touching the second dose of brandy, "on some stuff at the moment. And my next exhibition–"

"Is at the Firecrest Halls," supplied Aamon, "in January in the New Year."

"Yes."

"This commission of mine," said Aamon, with a lazy calm he did not at all feel, "is something *slightly* unusual."

"Oh, yes?" Torhec glanced at him. At no time so far had he properly *looked* at Aamon. Torhec seemed more interested in the vast views from the side windows. They were real ones, the vista of the Boulevard stretching for miles, railed in either side by the elegant and glassy buildings, and ending in the vanishing point of a winter sky. The sky too was wonderful, changed to royal purple by the morning lighting, and the city's Climate Control, whose soft wavering rays might sometimes be glimpsed shimmering above like the most self-effacing Northern Lights.

"What I had in mind," said Aamon, "is to commission from you one solitary piece–the subject to be anything you wish, of course, the choice is yours. And the *exhibition*, if so I can call it, would take place in my own house, the one here at the Heights. I expect you know the area."

"I've heard of it," said Torhec. "Very well. If that's what you'd like. When do you want it?"

Aamon thought, *We might as well be arranging a delivery of oranges, or a lawn-cutter. In a moment,* he thought, in a combination of rather childish glee and apprehension, *I shall wake up.*

"As soon as you can finish it," was all he said.

"No problem there, then. I have one or two new pieces already done provisionally for January. They won't miss them. If you don't care what you get, you can have one of those. My usual price–"

"We'll come to that," said Aamon. "Rest assured, the remittance will be extremely high, as befits your genius. And, as I've also said, to receive anything of yours will content me utterly. Would tomorrow be possible?"

Torhec abruptly grinned. His teeth were white and strong as the rest of him, as if purposely grown to help him *bite* his sculptures into being. "Why not? *Tonight,* if you like."

"I'd love it. This is splendid."

Torhec reached out, took the second brandy and downed it. He had half begun to get up again, the proffered financial reward seemingly almost immaterial to him, or else something of more import in the offing.

"Just one more thing," said Aamon, soothingly. "Perhaps you might sit down again, if you would. There is an additional matter I must put before you."

"Surely your people can let me know anything else. The payment too. I trust you, Van Glanz. You have a gloriously honest reputation. You've no reason anyway to cheat me. Simply get someone to arrange the details. Aside from that, you're aware of my own method. My work will be yours for one month, or one month and seven days if you want the fullest stretch. Then I shall arrive with my own people and, as always, I'll break everything up. It goes without saying, if you wish to invite guests also to witness that event, I have no objections. My own gang will then remove any debris. Nothing will mar your house or its furnishings, nor will any mote of my work remain."

"Precisely," said Aamon firmly. "Which is why I must enlighten you a little further."

Torhec sat. His face grew blank, and then a scowling concentration fixed it. For the first time he looked fully into Aamon's eyes, a disconcerting gaze, stony, Aamon thought, as any statue's–or a *gorgon's*. But the rich man was prepared.

"What I want, Torhec, is to *retain* your work indefinitely. I want it *not* to be broken up, as all your work always *is* broken up by you. By which you demonstrate the transience of loveliness, and life itself, your elegiac and practical reproof to God, or whatever ghastly supreme force makes and *breaks* all of us, and everything. I understand this, Torhec, and I *salute* it. But I, Torhec, also want to play at God, or at *a* god, a nicer one, who tries to save something fine from the wreck and give it–if only temporarily–the immortal life it deserves."

"No," said Torhec instantly, hard as a hammer blow.

"Wait," said Aamon, "let me finish. This exquisite work of yours–unknown by me so far, yet obviously exquisite because you have made it–will be kept in a vault of my house. The house at Heights has several such cellars. They are impenetrable, except by myself, or, in rare cases, those machines I prime with my authority. *No one*, Torhec, will have access to, or look at, your masterpiece, save me. I will swear this on or by any means you stipulate. If you wish you may examine all the arrangements. Only I, Torhec, *ever*, will see your work. This single work. I will even, if you wish, limit myself to a certain number of visits to it during any given year. There are ways of ensuring this. And you can check records of my dealings elsewhere. As you yourself have said, I have never reneged on any deal, never broken my word. I am known for that. Only *I* will ever regard this cherished creation. And, if you like, on my death it can be destroyed–remotely–by a charge laid in the vault." Aamon took one long, slow breath. He added, coolly, "And in return, I'll give you two million reulars."

Torhec's face, which had stayed like rock, now moved. Not only the eyes, but all of it seemed to *blink*.

He said nothing, but he swallowed. Much louder than when he drained the first brandy.

"Don't you think you're worth so much?" Aamon said. "Of course you do. Already you're becoming a wealthy man. But fashions alter, and even great genius may fall from its pedestal. We need only remember Mozart, or Clemorte Iyens. And too there is the unreliability of the world's currencies–always a little dubious now. Except the reular, which as everyone agrees, is the only safe monetary unit left. With two million of them, I'd think, you can do exactly as you please for the rest of your long, long extraordinary and creative life."

"I have been asked for this before. Nine times, and always by the very rich. I have always refused."

"Who offered you two million regulars?" Aamon asked, with the crude finesse of utter truth.

"None. I said, very rich, but not rich in your way, Van Glanz. But really it doesn't matter. My answer is the same. No."

They sat then in silence for a few moments. Aamon was more than aware that, despite the refusal, Torhec had not got up again to leave. Surreptitiously Aamon pressed the small button inside his sleeve that signalled to Brack, waiting in the corridor, that all was well. A sudden protective intrusion might be unhelpful.

Aamon tried to analyse Torhec's bleak and uncommunicative face. The man was staring again from the nearest window, studying perhaps the endless glittering traffic on the Boulevard. Considering?

Finally, Aamon spoke.

"Can I offer you more brandy? Or something else perhaps?"

"Aside from your money."

Torhec's tone was oddly bitter.

Wildly Aamon hoped to see in this a chink in the sculptor's granite walls. "Unfortunately, *my* only talent is to *make* money. I can't make anything else. Therefore it's all I *can* offer, aside from those necessities and luxuries money provides."

"I remain here," said Torhec, "because you puzzle me. Why do you want a piece of my work so much, if you propose showing it to no one else? What use is it to you? If you boast you have it, while you never reveal it, who'll believe you?"

"I told you. I respect your wish to reprimand a destructive God by copying Him. *I* want the role of a god who cherishes."

"You have a stock of treasures, no doubt."

"Some. Those I valued and could get."

"You must rate my work highly," said Torhec. And then–*then* he rose again to his feet. He drew on his coat.

"I have one last suggestion," said Aamon. And he too got up. He was rather shorter than Torhec, as he had known he must be. Next to the other's great hands his own looked like those of a boy of fourteen.

Torhec stood there. "Well?"

"If you will give me your work, in exchange for my two million reulars, I will agree, and under all former conditions as outlined, not only not to show the piece to any other, but *myself* not to look at it. *Never* to look at it. You shall put it in a crate, install a blind of some sort, an anti-X-ray filter to keep the interior of the container unseeable, seal it, lock it, *booby-trap* it if you wish. Ever unseen then, the contents will remain with me until my death, when–as I promised you–it shall be destroyed. And before that day or night it will, to all intents and purposes, remain invisible–non-existent–destroyed, *dead.* Like all your other work. No human eye will be set on it. No hand will touch it. I'll tell no one. Even those professionals who, monetarily, must be involved, will know nothing of the nature of the deal. Only I. I shall only–I shall only *know* it is there."

Torhec's face altered its contours. The most peculiar of smiles had crossed the rock. "Van Glanz," he said, "I believe you are as mad as I am."

The last month came, Endember, the month of the year's dying fire. Next came Christmas, and five days after, the New Year. At certain eras of life, both individual and general, time will move very swiftly. Further years arrived and, with their months and festivals, slid away into history. A fifth December ended, a fifth Endember began, just as always. It was once more Christmas Eve.

Veronise, who by then was the leading favourite among Aamon Van Glanz's seven mistresses, watched him with distinct inquisitiveness, which she did not attempt to disguise.

"You seem very edgy, darling," she said. "Is everything well with you?"

"Everything in my life is splendid, you most of all."

Knowing she had been fobbed off, Veronise gave him her wise-cat's smile.

Later, when they left the ivory-tinted bedroom and went downstairs for supper in the second, dark green, dining room, she was aware whatever it was that excited Aamon had not been quenched by love-making.

She did not question him now. She only went on

watching him.

He knew she did this, but her feline gaze had never troubled him.

When they reached the fruits and sweets stage of the meal, he said to her, "Have you ever heard, Vero, of the sculptor, Torhec?"

"Oh yes. I went to one of his shows once. A tiny piece of broken marble hit me in the face. I was only nineteen and I cried. My companion was very angry and afterward he told the officials there that people should be offered facial protection. It didn't scar me though, as you've seen."

Aamon looked at her consideringly. He was not amazed her main recollection of the event was that she had been hit by flying debris. It was pointless to ask if she had liked the sculptor's work.

"Five years ago," Aamon said, "I met Torhec."

"He was attractive," said Veronise, "in his own way."

"Perhaps. I thought him a genius. I still think this."

"I knew someone," said Veronise, slyly eating a Chinese peach, "who took a photograph of his statues. But the gallery police confiscated it. He had to pay a fine."

Aamon said, "I asked Torhec to sell me one of his works. I was willing to pay him two million reulars. Providing I could keep the work."

Veronise stopped eating. She raised her eyes and stared luminously right into his. She thought, *What should I do to make him offer me such a sum? Perhaps it might be possible.*

But she said, "What did he say?"

"He said no," Aamon replied.

"And did he mean it?"[!]

"Oh," said Aamon, "he must have. It was against his principles."

Principles, thought Veronise, *what in God's name are those?*

After a lavish cheese board they drank vitreous thimbles of a rare eastern spiced spirit, and returned to bed, this time in the crimson suite.

During the long winter night-morning, after 3 a.m., Aamon lay awake, his own brain ticking with little mouse-like scurrying thoughts, which, luckily, Veronise (a cat) would neither see nor sense.

He was well aware that he had a recurrent compulsion to tell people, occasionally *anyone,* about the deal he had firstly *wanted* to make, and then *attempted* to make, with Torhec. Needless to add that, once the deal was concluded, that end of December five years before, the urge to reveal it *all* to *anyone* had dogged him like the phantom hound of some preternatural curse.

Of course, despite constant flirtations, he resisted successfully and always. Part of his off-kilter delight in the deal's victory was this nagging joy of wanting to fling wide the doors of the secret and let it loose. But he had given his word. And he never broke his word, never betrayed or reneged. Such integrity was one of the huge pillars of his own personal achievement. He could not now afford to blab. Evidently, in the past, he had, with other things, never been tempted.

As it had been arranged between himself and Torhec, the manoeuvre was carried out like a kidnapping, or rather, the resolution of one, when the ransom is paid and the victim restored. Aamon had only obeyed the sculptor in this. Torhec had told him, as they sat again in the coffee-room of the exclusive club, exactly how everything must be done. He–Torhec–might have been planning it for days. Had he? Subsequently Aamon asked himself if that could be so. For Torhec might well have coined such a contingency modus operandi. Others after all had tried to buy the longevity of his work from him. If none offered such a succulent remuneration as Aamon, they had still proved that not even a Torhec might be completely free of pestering. (Every man too has his price. Or so they say. Inevitably the type of price may vary, not only in amount but in *scope.)*

Torhec outlined the procedure in a few cool sentences.

"One of my people will contact you inside the hour–or your agents, if you prefer. You or they will then meet him in person today–the place to be mutually arranged. Somewhere discreet."

"Why... yes," Aamon had murmured, docile, almost stunned.

"He will receive your cheque for the exact sum you've stipulated. Two million reulars."

"A–cheque–but the usual method of electronic transfer will see the money safely into your account, at any bank or freehouse of your choice, in moments–"

"No. I must insist on a cheque. Made out by your own hand, and likewise signed. An antiquated format I know, seldom used for over thirty years. But a man of your standing, Van Glanz, should have no difficulty in getting use of it."

"Yes, certainly then. A cheque. Why not–?"

"Once the cheque is in my possession, the artwork will be brought to you, by a couple of my work gang. Where do you want to take the delivery? At your agent's premises or directly at your house?"'

"My–" Aamon broke off. His breath had caught in his throat. He cleared it and said, "My house at the Heights."

"The piece will be invisibly stowed inside an ordinary box, a small wine crate. It won't look like anything at all. And it will also, in accordance with your promise, be X-ray filtered and sealed fast. You've sworn never to look at the piece, and you will be well advised not to try. As you said, you'll know it is there, an example of work by the sculptor Torhec, for the duration of your life. I advise you again now," Torhec added quietly, "never to break your word. *Never* to attempt to look. For your own sake."

His voice was devoid of any menace. It was flat and remote.

Aamon lowered his head. His wrists were trembling.

"Thank you," he said.

Then Torhec laughed at him. That was all: a brutal trio of barks. Torhec rose once more, and walked out of the room, and Aamon touched the hidden button in his sleeve in the summoning signal for Brack. By the time, nine seconds after, that the tall bodyguard entered, Aamon Van Glanz seemed quite composed. Within half an hour one of the most colossal freehouse bankers had been contacted. They had plenty of dealings with the Van Glanz corporation, and within a further twenty minutes everything was in motion.

Before the sun had even crossed behind the last quarter of the climate-controlled over-mantle, the large pale paper cheque, scrawled with jet-black words and numbers, had been couriered, offered, and accepted. Before the sun's blood-red ball had bounced entirely down under the horizon's edge, a small, stout wine-crate, normally the carriage for a dozen bottles of Fornian Pinot Blonde, had been unloaded in one of the inner halls of the Van Glanz mansion on Westnorth Heights.

Aamon stood alone with it in this hall for nearly an hour. He stood staring at the crate. Once he walked all round it, and then again: only twice.

Obviously, it had been sealed tight, and no doubt rigged with anti-tampering devices. It might even maim him or cost him his life should he attempt to open it. Or it would maim or kill anyone he designated to attempt that in his place. As for a machine making the attempt, doubtless that would result in an uncontrolled explosion, causing untold damage and also loss of life... But this did not even come into it. No, the threat of such a punishment was immaterial. He had given his word. And Torhec had trusted him.

Aamon Van Glanz was the only man, the only human on earth, who would now possess an artwork by Torhec the sculptor.

That must be enough.

The case was borne down into one of the lower vaults. In

a previous century it had been a bomb-shelter, and was reached by three individual elevators. The first was beautifully decorated, the second plain, and the third ugly, almost gross, and equipped only with a hideous Everlasting, one of the poisonous and dull light bulbs of that earlier period.

Aamon accompanied the porter robot that held the crate. Aamon oversaw its settlement in the long and narrow sub-basement chamber, whose walls were lined in platinum and lead. It sat there on the dark trestle, in the dull dead twilight, and stared back at him, and for another longish while he stood before it and gazed at its blank and unknowable face.

That night Aamon dreamed he came down in three stages from the mountain, behind Moses, who bore in his strong arms the two mighty tablets of stone on which the Laws of God had been inscribed. But both stones were blank, and Moses' brown eyes like the eyes of Torhec. So Aamon knew neither he, nor any other, would ever dare to ask, let alone try to decipher, the blank mystery of the Laws of God. They would all have to invent them, and even then they would risk both sanity and life by such temerity.

Those five years on, Aamon left the bed in the crimson suite, leaving Veronise, sleeping catlike.

He dressed in the adjacent annex, and went down through the house, got in turn into the three elevators, descending to the vault.

He alone knew the entry code. Even the machine that had first taken the crate there had had that portion of its memory erased.

Everything was just as he recalled. The light, the room, the box. There was no reason any of it should have been altered. But he had not gone back, not once in half a decade since the installation, and somehow he had believed (ridiculously), that some change *must* have occurred. Or he had only hoped so. Hoped that if he abstained from a visit for long enough, at last the wall of the casket might, spontaneously, have given way, and the wondrous prize be lying there naked, *visible.*

But the crate was as he had left it, the relatively germ-free moderated air, soured only by the Everlastings, stable and non-destructive to its material. Even the lettering, that told of twelve bottles of a sable-white wine, was pristine as if just printed on.

Aamon paced about the box. Round and round, far more than twice. He recalled the five-year-old dream, which he considered less blasphemous than crass. He thought of the myth of Pandora, who opened the forbidden box or chest or pitcher and let out all the evils of the world which–ever since–talented humanity had been striving to cram back.

And he thought too of the king in the other myth, with the ears of an ass, and of the barber–or whatever he had been–who had learned the secret and had to tell, in desperation whispering it to the river reeds. But ever after when the wind blew, or if any cut a reed and made a pipe, they sang the secret out loud. Asses' ears, asses' ears. *Asses' ears.*

Shall I tell just one? Aamon asked himself. *Not try to look, no, never that–simply... confide.* But to whom? To that woman upstairs? To some other woman? To a valued employee? To a drunk on the street?

Why did I come down here? I have the damnable thing. That is enough. I swore it would be. It is.

Torhec was by then in some foreign country. He still gave his exhibitions. Was still well-known, feted, scorned, criticised, and adored. Now whole arenas were filled by people on those final days of the Armageddons–the "closing ceremonies"; when everything was smashed and melted into crumble and clinker. Huge screens sometimes relayed the proceedings to those outside who had been unable to obtain, or afford, a seat. (The tapes that supplied the screens were always, it went without saying, presently wiped.)

But Torhec would have no need to worry now if ever his prowess waned. A great if eccentric star, he would be safe for the duration of his days, having those riches Aamon had given him. While Aamon himself, of course, had never missed the two million, amid the opulence of his personal fortune.

I have it. I have it. That is enough. There it is. When all the rest is gone, when he has destroyed all of that, this is here with me, while I live. It's mine.

He went back up through the house, and undoing a high window in a lonely room, whispered into the ecologically selective light snow now spinning down through the climate-controlling waves above, "I have a piece by Torhec, Torhec. *Torhec.*"

Inside eleven further years, Aamon Van Glanz passed from the rank of multinaire. He became a max-multinaire, one of the wealthiest men on the planet.

All that happened without his lifting a finger, accepting a contributory call, scanning an apposite viewer. Without, in a curious manner, his really noticing.

While, in the same way, he began to grow old, also barely noticing.

That is, it crept up on him, his aging. Just as his wealth had done. Two panthers stalking him, the first golden and gleaming, limber and imperious. The second grey, deadly, sad.

That particular Endember, he was at the other, older, northern house, by the sea.

Out in the wilds, there was no Climate Control, except what had been introduced into the building. Heavy snow had fallen, a blazing white even in the gathering dusk, and fringes of the ocean had frozen into a thickly-striated weave of ice. Beyond, bluish milk, the water stretched to the matte blue band of vision's end.

Reflected in a fifty-foot high pane of window, Aamon

could see his last mistress, Ezessi, calmly knitting a shapeless mass of coppery wool.

"Tomorrow," he said, "I think I'll be returning to the Heights."

She did not pause. "Of course. Shall I come with you?"

"Yes, please do. It's much warmer there–I mean it *looks* much warmer. When I was young, Zess, I used to spend a whole twenty-eight day winter month here, staring out at that view. But now, now..." He did not finish.

In the window her reflection glanced up at him, gently, and forbearingly. She was not a vast amount younger than he. Perhaps she understood that, in some incoherent form, he feared the coldness of the landscape, and the sea, might one day trap his ousted soul or personality; he would then wander forever on the frigid shore. He had better be very careful and never die, here.

During the afternoon Aamon had watched Torhec on the WWV. Sometimes Aamon dialled the searcher to find out where the sculptor was, and now and then had been rewarded, if such was the proper phrase, by a handful of minutes broadcast live from one of Torhec's "closing ceremonies". These were the things everyone always wanted to see, although the briefest whirl of images from the latest exhibited and doomed works (under contract all footage to be destroyed less than ten seconds following the hammer blow) flashed by, before the mayhem began.

Torhec too had grown older through the years. He appeared, unsurprisingly, well-off. Yet he was still, both physically and psychically, a carelessly powerful man. A little thickening at the waist, a slight laxness of facial muscle. They did not detract, would only have been truly notable to such a connoisseur as Aamon Van Glanz. The sculptor's eyes stayed dark and focused. His dark hair merely had been seeded, like the northern ocean, with ice. There was a small thin scar on his other cheek. But his hands carried no spots of age. They remained huge, fine, and lethally capable.

By then, that afternoon, Aamon was so used to watching Torhec's destructions they had, Aamon believed, slight effect on him. He had never, after the initial visit, gone to any other of the exhibitions.

Ezessi and he dined in the closed dining room, which had no windows, and which played its human occupants Bach. After this they went to their separate beds. It was Ezessi's company he relished now the most. Should he feel any other need it was more easily satisfied alone. And that mostly to please his physician, who had assured him sexual release was good for him in moderation.

The next day, he and she flew out through a white blanket of weather and into a dark, bony evening. By 4 p.m. they were in the mansion at the Heights. Real logs burned in the grates. All the lamps were lit.

"Zess," he said, countless times, always instantly breaking off and changing the subject....

When dinner was done she said to him, "What's troubling you, Aamon, my dear?" He had never known with any of his women how sincere they were–generally his common sense had told him: not very. But Ezessi had this unusual sibylline calm. She was very nearly as serene as an icon.

Aamon poured them another après-fin and sat down in his chair.

"Some years ago," he said, looking only into the shallow tulip of green liqueur, "I bought a piece of art from Torhec. You know who I mean by Torhec?"

"Yes, my dear. You've told me about him. We've often watched him on the world wide view. In fact, just yesterday, we did so."

"I hadn't forgotten, Zess."

"Did I say you had, Aamon?"

"The point is—I *kept* the work I bought from him. I *kept* it." He added, as if to the drink alone, *"Kept it."*

"So he didn't destroy it, as apparently he always must."

"No, Zess. I persuaded him. We did a deal. But I swore I'd tell no one. Now I have. You." Aamon waited. She said nothing. Her serene face lured him on. "And anyway, the core of our agreement was that I was *never* to look at the artwork he'd given me. I never saw it before either. He sealed it in a crate. *I* suggested it could be booby-trapped. It's been here, under this house, ever since. About two miles down."

"In the old bomb-shelter."

"An iota lower than that."

"It seems, Aamon, not unreasonable."

"What do you mean? Of course it's *madness.* To have bought it–and never–*seen it.*"

"Did you never before," she mildly inquired, "buy something that you did not see?"

"Stocks–economic portals–items of my so-called financial empire. Yes, those. Houses even. This house I bought through an agent, and never bothered to view the report. But such things–in any case, I did eventually see them all, or the results they brought. But the work of art Torhec sold me–sight unseen and never seen. I think now I really must. Tonight. It will be now."

She appeared to be studying him attentively.

At last she said, "What about the booby-trap?"

"Oh," he said plaintively. "I sent an expert team in while we were in the north. They checked the crate by machine. Then two volunteers personally tested it. It seems, rather strangely, they're often asked to carry out such services, test the opening of things without themselves actually breaking the vessel undone. Once or twice members of the team have died, doing such work, but their dependents are always excessively compensated. Besides, they have assured me, Torhec's crate is locked only with an ordinary electrolock. There are no devices at all rigged on or inside it. There's only the filter, of course, to prevent anyone seeing its interior through an X-ray camera or similar intrusion."

Aamon paced about the room. "I could have undone the thing and looked at it at any time during all these–what is it? –fifteen, sixteen years. The very day after he sent it to me. That night. I could have looked then. I never did."

"Why not?" Her voice was like his own inner voice. It had asked him too: *Why not? As* he had answered himself, he answered her. "I'd sworn not to: I don't break my word. Never have. I'm *famous* for this. But that wasn't the reason."

"What was?"

"I don't know. Not fully. Why I *didn't* look, why I *must* look now."

He had reached one of the windows of the house at the Heights, and gazed down on the glittering firefly heap of the city so far below. On to this view her reflection was not projected, nor really his.'

Softly he heard her ask, "Aamon, are you ill?"

"Oh–no. No, not at all–not yet. But I suppose getting old has something to do with this. Because he–Torhec is like *God.* He creates and mercilessly destroys. I have to have some kind of *answer*–even though I don't know what the answer is, or even if there can *be* an answer."

She said, "Torhec only reminds me of that priest who sponsored the burning of great works of art during the Renaissance in Italy. I think his name was Savonarola. He called the destruction the *Bonfire of the Vanities.*"

But Aamon had barely heard her finally. He did not see the room, or his reflection, or the city outside. Already, mentally, he was in the first elevator, travelling smoothly down into the abyss below.

Above him, on the ceiling of that first elevator, when physically he reached it, was painted a sunshined summery sky. Never before had this struck him as incongruous; no doubt he had not been paying attention. Oddly, now his concentration seemed fixed like steel elsewhere, he did take in everything rather sharply. For example the swift glide of the first lift's motion down, and the somewhat slower gait of the second. The third and last went extremely quickly. It made his stomach churn a moment, or that was only perhaps his nerves.

Once in the under-room, bathed in the awful Everlasting light, Aamon approached the box rapidly. Those others, sanctioned by him, frisked by the new bodyguard, Slait, monitored by robots, had used the lifts and entered here not long ago, to perform their tests. But even now the space seemed undisturbed, and on the side of the crate, black as if just applied, the spurious identity; *Pinot Blonde (Zibeline Blanche) 12.*

A suitable key to the electrolock had already been extrapolated from the lock template, fashioned, and left for Aamon's collection in a robotic safe that would reply only to his thumbprint. Now it did so, its mindless penetrating eye gleaming.

For a second then, holding the key, he faltered. He was not afraid, he discovered, not excited. He was anxious, and–deeply unhappy. Oh, not because of any guilt, not because he broke his oath. Be damned to that. He was allowed, surely, one blot on his inconsequent virtue. What was it, then? Standing with the key, which winked its own wicked little white light, leaden sorrow washed through him.

He would be disappointed, that must be it. He was having a premonition of seeing, in the opened crate, some unimportant work Torhec had palmed off on a rich idiot. Or of abruptly realising, after all the years of spellbound recollection, that after all Torhec was now hopelessly behind the times, or–worse–had never been any good. In the box then would be an inferior lump of rubbish, retained so long, and in such mesmeric captivity. As if Aamon had bravely swarmed the castle of the Sleeping Beauty, only to find an unexceptional if rather coarse female, snoring, or more repugnantly, *waking up,* and reaching out demanding hands.

Aamon shrugged off the weight of all this, the unease,

the superstition, and his grief.

With due care he applied the key to the lock.

Which gave a caustic little click.

Perhaps, despite everything, the crate would now explode.

But the crate did not do anything save give the slightest quiver. The near side of it slipped about a quarter of an inch out of the securing groove. It was open. From the narrow line of darkness, caused mostly by the X-ray-deterring filter, came a faint walnutty smell, and a whisper of the filmiest particles–dust.

Then he felt he could not move. Then, unavoidably, he moved.

Aamon Van Glanz wrenched out the side panel of Pandora's Box, (wood splintered, the filter cracked), and the drizzle of the miserly Everlasting light soaked in.

Staring at his revelation, the maxmultinaire said–thought –nothing. Only after a while he burst into a bellowing shout. When the shout ended, once again he stood entranced. It was very likely another hour before he leant forward and reached inside the crate.

Aamon woke Ezessi in the long winter night. He did this with apology, and a bottle of vintage champagne the colour of mercury. She knew it was not sex he required. Those nights had passed.

"My dear, what is it?"

"Oh. It's victory, Zess."

She waited.

He said, "For something."

They drank the first glass. There was plenty. It was a jeroboam.

"I went," he said, "to the crate. I opened it."

"Yes," she murmured when he stopped, as if seeming to wait for her avowal of remembering. And next, when again he seemed to await her prompt, "And what was there? Was it—beautiful?"

"Yes, it was quite beautiful, in its own terrible, horrible, cruel, and heartless way."

"He had–" even she hesitated, "he had somehow arranged that it be destroyed when you undid the crate?"

"No, my love. He'd destroyed it even before it went *into* the crate. He knew–he *must* have known–he knew what I did *not* know then–that one day I must *look*. Such was his power over me. And so he arranged it that, if I *should* look, I would find only the destruction. Demonstrably, if I'd kept my bloody word, I would never have known what lay inside the box. I could have retained my peerless illusion instead that I possessed one isolated masterpiece which had survived his onslaught."

They drank a second glass, very slowly.

He asked her, "Aren't you curious as to what it might have been? I mean, what the *rubble* amounted to–powdered stone, or chips of wood, or the stain of acid."

"Please tell me, Aamon," she said, patiently.

Now he felt himself so alone, Aamon did not find her patience either irritating or consoling.

As if randomly he said, "It occurred at once to me that I *do* in fact possess one of Torhec's masterpieces, since I have the *remains* of something he destroyed. Normally, every bit is cleared away, disposed of. But for this he'll have worn gloves. Or even–my God–even made someone else complete the job. Yes. That's what he'd do. So not a print, not a trace of DNA is there. Nothing of his. Nothing. Yet too I *know* this thing, even in its ruin. Frankly it wasn't really his, though it would have been. *I'd seen it once.* Sixteen years ago. *He* hadn't *made* it."

She watched him. Was she startled?

Aamon closed his eyes. He continued. "They're unusual, of course. But I've used them, here and there. It was my cheque to him, you see. The cheque that paid him for his work. Torn into two million pieces, one for each of the reulars–or so it looked. That's what was in the crate."

Observing him now, Ezessi saw his face had voided all expression. How empty he seemed. His was a mask she had glimpsed occasionally on the WWV, the face of a man whose skull had been smashed, still alive yet lobotomised, feeling nothing, and never to feel much ever again.

He put down his glass and said, in a sort of clockwork voice, "One day Torhec himself will vanish. Like all of us. They'll find *his* debris. It will be laughing. He, if none of the rest of us, has understood the joke."

Doll Re Mi

Folscyvio saw the Thing in a small cramped shop off the Via Silvia. In fact, he almost passed it by. He had just come from the Laguna, climbed the forty mildewy, green-velveted steps to the Ponte Louro and so crossed over to the elevated arcades of the Nuova. Then he glanced down, and spotted Giavetti, who owed him money, creeping by below through the ancient alleys. Having called and not been heard–or been ignored–Folscyvio descended quickly. But on entering the alley he saw Giavetti was gone, (or had hidden). Irritated, Folscyvio walked the alley, clicking his teeth together. And something with a rich wild colour slid by his right eye. At first his attention was not captured. But then, having walked a few more steps, Folscyvio's mind, as he would have put it, tapped him on the shoulder: *Look back, Maestro*! And there behind the flawed and watery window-glass, hung about by old, plum-coloured bannerets and thick cobwebs, was the peculiar Thing. He stood and stared at it for quite five minutes before going into the shop.

He was, Folscyvio, of medium height, but seemed taller due to his extreme leanness. His was a handsome face, aquiline, and reminiscent, as was more genuinely much of the city, of The Past. His hair was very long, very dark and thick and heavily if naturally curled. His eyes, long-lashed and bright, were narrow and of an alluring, or curious–or *repellent*–greyish-mauve.

No one was immediately attendant in the shop. Folscyvio poised for some while inside the open window-space, staring at the Thing. In the end he stepped near and examined a paper which had been pinned directly beneath.

Not many words were on the paper, these written old-fashionedly by hand, and in black ink: *Vio-Sera. A vio-sirenalino. From the Century 17. A rare example. Attributable, perhaps, to the Messers Stradivari.*

Folscyvio scowled. He did not for an instant credit this. Yet the Thing did indeed seem antique. Certainly, it was a *sort* of violin. But–but...

The form was that of a woman, from the crown of the head to her hips, the area just between the navel and the feminine pudenda. After which, rather than legs, she possessed the tail of a fish. She was made of glowing auburn wood–he was unsure of its type. All told, the figure, including the tail, was not much more than half a metre in length.

It had a face, quite beautiful in a stark and static kind of way, and huge eyes, each of which had been set with white enamel, and then, at the iris with a definitely fake emerald, having a black enamel pupil. Its mouth was also enamelled, pomegranate red. The image had breasts too, full and proud of themselves, with small strawberry enamel nipples. In the layers of the carved tail had been placed tiny discs of greenish, semi-opaque crystal. Some were missing, inevitably. Even if not a product of the Stradivari, nor quite so mature as the 1600s, this piece had been around for some time. The two oddest features were firstly, of course, the strings that ran from the finger board of the piscean tail, across the gilded bridge to the string-clasper, which lay behind a gilded shell at the doll's throat; while the nut and tuning pegs made up part of the tail's finishing fan. Secondly, what was odd was the *hair*, this not carved nor enamelled, but a fluid lank heavy mass, like dead brown silk, that flowed from the wooden scalp and meandered down, ending level, since the doll was currently upright, where, had the tail constituted legs, its knees might have been.

A grotesque and rather awful object. A fright, and a sham too, as it must be incapable of making music. For the third freakish aspect was, obviously, at the moment the doll *was* upright. But when the instrument–if such were even possible–was *played* what then? Aside from the impediment of its slightness yet encumberedness, the welter of hair–perhaps once that of a living woman, now a hundred years at least dead?–would slide, when the doll was upside-down, into everything, tangling with the strings and their tuning, the player's hands and fingers–his *throat* even, the bow itself.

Thinking this, Folscyvio abruptly noted there were also omissions from the creature, for she, this unplayable mermaid- violin, this circus-puppet, this con-trick, had herself neither arms nor hands. A mythic cripple. Just as he had thought she might render her player. Another man, he thought, would already loathe her, and be on his way out of the shop.

But it went without saying Folscyvio was of a different sort. Folscyvio was unique.

Just then, a thin stooped fellow came crouching out of some lair at the back of the premises.

"Ah, Signore. How may I help you?"

"That Thing," said Folscyvio, in a flat and slightly sneering tone.

"Thing... Ah. The vio-sera, Signore?"

"*That.*" Folscyvio paused, frowning, yet fastidiously amused. "It's a joke, yes?"

"No, Signore."

"*No*? What else can it be but a joke? Ugly. Malformed. And such a claim! My God. The *Stradivari.* How is it ever to be played?"

The stooped man, who had seemed very old and perhaps was not, necessarily, gazed gently at this handsome un-customer. "At dusk, Signore."

Even Folscyvio was arrested.

"*What*? At dusk - what do you mean?"

"As the fanciful abbreviation has it–*vio-sera*–a violin for evening, to be played when shadows fall. The Silver Hour between the reality of day and the mysterious mask of night. The hour when ghosts are seen."

Folscyvio laughed harshly, mockingly, but his brain was already working the idea over. A concert, one of so many he had given, displaying his genius before the multitude of adoring fanatics–sunset, dusk–the tension honeyed and palpable– *chewable* as rose-petal lakoum–

"Oh, then," he said. Generously contemptuous: "Very well. We'll let that go. But surely, whoever botched this rubbish up, it was never the Famiglia Stradivarius."

"I don't know, Signore. The legend has it, it was a son of that family."

"Insanity."

"She was, allegedly, one of three such models, our vio-sirenalino. But there is no proof of this, or the maker, you will understand, Signore. Save for one or two secret marks still visible about her, which I might show you. They are in any case, Masonic. You might not recognise them."

"Oh, you think not?"

"Then, perhaps you might."

"Why anyway," said Folscyvio, "would you think me at all seriously interested?"

The stooped old-young man waited mildly. He had whitish, longish hair. His eyes were dark and unreadable.

"Well," said Folscyvio, grinning, "just to entertain me, tell me what price you ask for the Thing? If you do ask one. A curiosity, not an instrument–perhaps it's only some adornment of your shop." And for the very first he glanced about. Something rather bizarre, then. Dusty cobwebs or lack of light seemed to close off much of the emporium from his gaze. He could not be certain of what he now squinted at, (with his gelid, grey-mauve eyes). Was it a collection of mere oddities–or of other instruments? Over there, for example, a piano... or was it a street-organ? Or *there*, a peculiar vari-coloured railing–or a line of flutes... Folscyvio took half a step forward to investigate. Then stopped. Did this white-haired imbecile know who the caller was? Very likely. Folscyvio was not unfamous, nor his face unknown. A redoubtable musician, a talent far beyond the usual. *Fireworks and falling stars*, as a prestigious publication had, not ten weeks before, described his performance both in concert halls and via Teleterra.

Suddenly Folscyvio could not recall what he had said last to the old-young mental deficient. Had he asked a price?

Or–what *was* it?

When confused or thrown out of his depth, Folscyvio could become unreasonable, unpleasant. Several persons had found this out, over the past eighteen years. His prowess as a virtuoso was such that, generally, excuses were made for him and police bribed, or else clever and well-paid lawyers would subtly 'usher' things away.

He stared at the ridiculous auburn wood and green glass of the fish-tail, at the pegs of brass and ivory adhering to the glaucous tail-fan.

He said, with a slow and velvety emphasis, "I'm not saying I want to buy this piece of crap off you. But I'd better warn you, if I *did* want, I'd get it. And for a–shall I say–very *reasonable* price. Sometimes people even *give* me things, as a present. You see? A diamond the size of my thumb-nail–quite recently, that. Or some genuine gold Roman coins, Circa Tiberio. Just *given*, as I said. A *gift*. I have to add, my dear old gentleman, that when people upset me, I myself know certain... *other* people, who really dislike the notion that I'm unhappy. They then, I'm afraid, do these unfortunate things–a broken window–oh, steelglass doesn't stop them–a little fire somewhere. The occasional, *very* occasional, broken... bone. Just from care of me, you'll understand. Such kind sympathy. *Do you know who I am*?"

The slightest pause.

"No, Signore."

"Folscyvio."

"Yes, Signore?"

"*Yes.*" Oh, the old dolt was acting, effecting ignorance. Or maybe he was blind and half-deaf as well as stooped. "So. How fucking much?"

"For the vio-sirenalino?"

"For what fucking else, in this hell-hall of junk?"

Folscyvio was shouting now. It surprised him slightly. Why did he care? Some itch to try, and to conquer, this stupid toy eyesore– Besides, he could afford millions of libra-eura. (Folscyvio did not know he was a miser of sorts; he did not know he was potentially criminally violent, an abusive and trustless, perhaps an evil man. Talent he had, great talent, but it was the flare and flame of a cunning stage magician. He could play instruments both stringed and keyed, with incredible virtuosity–but also utter emotional dryness. His greatest performances lacked all soul–they were fire and lightning, glamour and glitter, sound and fury. Signifying nothing? No, Folscyvio did not know any of *that* either. Or... he thought he did not, for from where, otherwise, the groundless meanness, the lashing out, the rage?)

Unusually, the stooping man did not seem unduly alarmed. "Since the need is so urgent," he said, "naturally, the vio-sera is yours. At least," a gentle hesitation, "for now."

"Forget 'for now'," shouted Folscyvio. "You won't get the Thing back. How much?"

"Uno lib'euro."

Everything settled to a titanic silence.

In the silence Folscyvio took the single and insignificant note from his wallet, and let it flutter down, like a pink-green leaf, into the dust of the floor.

The enormous lamp-blazing stadium, fretted by goldleafery and marble pillars, with a roof seemingly hundreds of metres high, and rock-caved with acoustic-enhancing spoons and ridges, roared and rang like a golden bell.

It had been a vast success, the concert. But they always were. The cheapest ticket would have cost two thousand. Probably half a million people, crushed luxuriously onto their velvet perches like be-jewelled starlings, during the performance rapt or sometimes crying out in near orgasmic joy, were now exploding in a final release that had less to do with music than... frankly, *with* release. One could not sit for three hours in such a temple and before such a god as Folscyvio, and not require, ultimately, some personal eruption. They were of all ages. The young mingled freely with those of middle years, and those who were quite old. All, of course, were rich, or incredibly rich. One did not afford a Folscyviana unless one was. Otherwise, there were the disks, sound only as a rule, each of which would play for three hours, disgorging the genius pyrotechnics of Folscyvio's hands, all those singing and swirling strings of notes, pearl drops of piano keys. Sometimes, even included on a disk, since a feature, often, of the show, the closing auction, and the sacrifice. The notes of *that*, (though they were *not* notes), faultlessly reproduced: the stream-like ripple, the flicker of a holy awakening, the *other* music, and then the *other* roar, the dissimilar applause, very unlike, if analysed, the bravos and excelsiors that were rendered earlier.

Oddly though, these perfect disk recordings did not ever, completely, (for anyone), capture the thrill of being present, of *watching* Folscyvio, as he played. Even the very rare, and authorised, visuals did not. If anything, such records seemed rather–flat. Rather–soulless. Indeed, only the bargaining and sacrifice that occasionally concluded the proceedings truly came across as fully exciting. Strange. Other artists were capturable. Why not the magnificent Folscyvio? But naturally, his powers were elusive, unique. There was none like him.

For those in the stadium, they were not considering disks, or anything at all. They knew, as the concert was over, there was every likelihood of that *second* show.

Look, see now, Folscyvio was raising his hand to hush them. And in his arm still he held the little vioncello, the very last instrument he had performed upon tonight.

Colossal quiet fell like a curtain.

Beyond the golden stadium and its environs, hidden by its windowlessness, the edges of the metropolis lay, and the Laguna staring silver at the moonlit sea. But in here, another world. Religious, yet sadistic. Sacred, yet–as some critic had coined it–savage as the most ancient rites of prehistory.

Then the words, so well known. Folscyvio:"Shall we have the auction, my friends?"

And a roiling cheer, unmatched to any noise before, shot high into the acoustic caves.

The *Bidding For* began at two thousand–the cheapest seat-price. The *Bidding Against* sprang immediately to four thousand. After this, the bids flew swift and fierce, carried by the tiny microphones that attended each plushy perch.

For almost half an hour the factions warred. The *Yes* vote rose to a million scuta-euri. The *No* vote flagged. And then the Maestro stilled them all again. He told them, with what the journals would describe as his 'wicked lilt' of a smile, that after all, he had decided perhaps it should not be tonight. No, no, my friends, my children, (as the vociferous and more affluent *Yeses* trumpeted disappointment) not *this* time, not *now*. This time–is out of joint. Perhaps, *next* time. This night we will have a stay of execution.

And then, in a further tempest of frustrated disagreement and adoring hosannas, Folscyvio, still carrying the vioncello, left the stage.

"But what are you doing *there*, Folscy-mio?"

Uccello the agent's voice was laden with only the softest reproach. He knew well to be careful of his prime client; so many of Folscyvio's best agents had been fired, and one or two, one heard, received coincidental injuries.

Yet Folscyvio seemed in a calm and good-humoured mood.

"I came to the coast, dear Ucci, to learn to play."

"To–to *learn*? *You*? The *Maestro*–but you know everything there is to–"

"Yes, *yes*." One found Folscyvio could become impatient with compliments, too. One must be careful even there. "I mean the new Thing."

"Ah," said Uccello, racking his brains. Which new thing? Was it a piano? No–some sort of violin, was it not? "The–mermaid," he said cautiously.

"Well done, Ucci. Just so. The ugly nasty wrongly-sized little upside-down mermaid doll. She is quite difficult, but I find ways to handle her."

Uccello beamed through the communicating connection. Folscyvio, he knew, found ways often to cope with females. (Uccello could not help a fleeting sidelong memory of buying off two young women that Folscyvio had 'slapped around', in fact rather severely. Not to mention the brunette who claimed he had raped her, and who meant to sue him, before–quite astonishingly–she disappeared.)

"Anyway, Ucci, I must go now. Ciao alia parte."

And the connection was no more.

Well, Uccello told himself, pouring another ultra-strong coffee, whatever Folscyvio did with the weird violin, it would make them all lots of money. Sometimes he wished Folscyvio did not make so much money. Then it would be easier to let go of him, to escape from him. Forever.

He had found the way to deal with her infuriating hair. Of course he could have cut it off or pulled it out. But it was so indigenous to her flamboyant grotesquery he had decided to retain it if at all possible. In the end the coping strategy came clear.

He drew all the hair up to the top of the wooden scalp, and there secured it firmly with a narrow titanium ring. This kept every fibre away from his hands, and the bow, once he had upended her and tossed the full cascade back over his left shoulder, well out of his way. Soon others, at his terse instruction, had covered the titanium in thick fake gold, smooth and non-irritant. Only then did he have made for her a bow. It was choice. What else, being for his use.

As for the contact-point, it had been established thus: her right shoulder rested between his neck and jaw. Now he could control her, he might begin.

By then she had been carefully checked, the strings found to be new and suitable and well-tended, resilient. He himself tuned them. To his momentary interest they had a sheer and dulcet sound, a little higher than expected, while from the inner body a feral resonance might be coaxed. She was so much better than Folscyvio had anticipated.

After all this, he adapted to his normal routine when breaking in a novel piece.

He rose early and took a swim in the villa pool, breakfasted on local delicacies, then set to work alone in the quartet of rooms maintained solely for the purpose. Here he worked until lunch, and after siesta resumed working in the evening.

The house lay close to the sea, shut off from the town, an outpost of the city. In the dusk, as in the past, he would have gone down to the shore and taken a second swim in the water, blue as syrup of cobalt. But now he did not. However pleased with, or aggravated by, the mermaid he might have become, at twilight he would always play her. He had not, it seemed, been entirely immune to the magical idea that she was a vio-sera, a violin of the Silver Hour.

It was true. She did have a fascination for him. He *had* known this, he thought, from the moment he glimpsed her in the sordid little shop off the Via Silvia. He had become fascinated by instruments before in this manner, as, very occasionally, by girls. It happened less now, but was exciting, both in rediscovery, and its power. For as with all such affairs of his, involving music, or the romantic lusts of the body, he would be the only Master. And at the finish of the flirtation, the destroyer also.

By night, after a light dinner, he slept consistently soundly.

The Maestro dreamed.

He was walking on the pale shore beside the sea, the waves black now and edged only by a thin sickle moon. At spaces along the beach, tall, gas-fired cressets burned, ostensibly to mimic Ancient Roma. Folscyvio was indifferently aware that, due to these things, he moved between the four elements: earth, and water, fire and air.

Then he grew conscious of a figure loitering at the sea's border, not far from him.

In waking life, Folscyvio would have kept clear of others on a solitary walk–which anyway, despite his wished-for aloneness, always saw, in a spot like this, one of his bodyguards trailing about twenty metres behind him. Now, however, no guard paced in tow. And an immediate interest in the loiterer made Folscyvio alter course. He idled down to the unravelling fringes of the tideless waves, and when the figure turned to him, it was as if this meeting had been planned for weeks.

No greeting, even so, was exchanged.

Aside from which, Folscyvio could not quite make out who–even, really, *what*–the figure was. Not very tall, either bowed or bundled down into a sort of dark hooded coat, the face hidden, perhaps even by some kind of webby veil.

Most preposterously, none of this unnerved Folscyvio. Rather, it seemed all correct, exactly right, like recognising, say, a building or tract of land never before visited, though often regarded in a book of pictures.

Then the figure spoke. "Giavetti is dead."

"Ah, good. Yes, I was expecting that. Has the debt been recovered?"

"No," said the figure.

It was a gentle, ashy voice. Neither male or female, just as the form of it seemed quite asexual.

"Well, it hardly matters," said Folscyvio who, in the waking world, would have been extremely put out.

"But the death," said the figure, "all deaths that have been deliberately caused, they do matter."

"Yes, yes, of course," Folscyvio agreed, unconcerned yet amenable to the logic of it.

"Even," said the figure, "the death of *things*."

Folscyvio was intrigued. "Truly? How diverting. Why?"

"All things are constructed," the figure calmly said, and now, just for a second, there showed the most lucent and mellifluous gleam of eyes, "constructed, that is, from the same universal, partly psychic material. A tree, a man, a lion, a wall–we are all the same, in that way."

"I see," said Folscyvio, nodding. They were walking on together, over the shore, the waves melting in about their feet, and every so often a fiery cresset passing, as if it walked in the other direction, casting out splinters of volcanic tangerine glass on the wrinkles of the water.

"You are an animist," said the figure. "You do not understand this in yourself, but you sense a life-force in every instrument on which you set your hands. And being sufficiently clever to recognise the superior life in them, you are jealous, envious and vengeful." There was no disapproval, no anger in the voice, despite what it had said, or now said. "To a human who is *not* a murderer, the destruction of life is crucially terrible, whether the life of a man, a woman, or a beast. To an animist these events are also terrible, but, too, the slaughter of so-called *objects* is equally a horror, an abomination–a tree, a wall–and especially those objects which can speak or sing. And worse still, which have spoken and sung–for the one who kills them. A piano. A violin.

"A violin," repeated Folscyvio, and a warm and stimulating pleasure surged up in him, reminiscent, though physically unlike, the sparkle of erotic arousal. "A *violin*."

Then he noticed they had reached the end of the shoreline. How strange: nothing lay beyond, only the gigantic sky, scattered with stars, and open as the sea had seemed to be moments before. Although the sea, evidently, had been contained by a horizon. As this was not.

Folscyvio worked with the doll-mermaid-violin, mostly sticking to his routine, where departing from it then compensating with a fuller labour in the day or night which followed. (During this time he discovered no secret marks, Masonic or otherwise, on its surface. But of course, the shop-keeper had lied.)

Three, then four months passed. The weather-control that operated along the coast maintained blissful weather, only permitting some rain now, at the evening hour of the Aperitivo.

He ordered Uccello to cancel a single concert he had been due to give in the city. Uccello was appalled. "Oh never fear, they'll forgive me. Change the venue of my next one, to make room for those worshippers who missed out." Folscyvio knew he *would* be forgiven. He was a genius. One must allow him room to act as he wished. Only those who hated and despised him ever muttered anything to the contrary. And they–and Folscyvio knew this also well–would be careful what they said, and where. It was well known, Folscyvio's fanatics did not take kindly to his defamation.

Without a doubt, beyond all question, he had mastered her. It was the beginning of the fifth month. He stood in front of a wide mirror (his habitual act prior to a performance) and put himself, in slow-motion, through his various flourishes, emotives, intensities, particularly those that were intrinsic to the new and extraordinary instrument. Already he had formulated the plan for her deployment and display before he should–finally, and after prevarication–take hold of her. She was to preside, to start with, at the off-centre front stage. She would then be upright, that was the *doll* appearance of her would be the most obvious. Her hair would pour from the gold tiara, carefully arranged about and over her breasts, her face smooth and glowing from preparatory days of polishing, her emerald eyes, (also polished), shining and her pomegranate lips inviting. She would be standing on her aquatic tail, in which all the missing scales by now were replaced. The fan-tail base of it would balance on a velvet cushion of the darkest green. Magnetic beams would hold her infallibly in position. (The insurance paid for this, not to mention the threats issued, both legal and otherwise, would make certain all was well.)

After posing and scrutinizing all his moves and postures, Folscyvio played to the mirror the selected pieces on the vio- sera, as he proposed to at the forthcoming concert now only two weeks away. Everything went faultlessly, of course.

Sometimes he would be assisted, during a concert, by an accompanying band, comprising percussion, certain stringed instruments, a small horn section, and so on. All these accoutrements were robotic; he never employed human musicians. The Maestro himself always checked the ensemble over, tuned and–as a favourable critic had expressed it– '*exalted*' them for a show. However, on this occasion, when he reached the moment that he accessed the vio-sirenalino, (the Mermaid, as she had been billed), the exquisite little robot band would fall quite silent. At which, being non-human, no flicker of envy would disturb any morsel of it.

Then, and only then, at a signal from the Maestro, ultra-protective rays would spin the mermaid violin, whirling her to her true position, upside down.

Folscyvio, amid the crowd's predicted applause and uproar, would lift her free. Like a heroine in some swooning novel of the nineteenth, twentieth, or early twenty-first Century, she would lie back upon his shoulder, her hair drifting in a single silken, burnt-sienna wing down his back, (the hair had been refurbished, too). In this fainting and acquiescent subjection of hers he would hold her, and bring the slender bow to bear upon her uptilted, supine body, stroking, spangling, *making love* to her, breasts to tail.

In the wide mirror he could see now, even if he had already known, the eroticism of this act. How gorgeously perverse. How sublime. How *they* would love it. And oh, the music she could make–

For her tones *were* beautiful. They were–*unique*. And only he, master of his art, had brought her to this. Even that dolt Uccello, hearing a brief example, a shred of Couperin, a skein of Vivaldi, and of Strarobini, played, recorded and audioed through the speaker, had exclaimed, "But–Folscymio–never did I hear you play anything–with quite this *vividity*. What enchantment. Folscyvio, you have found your true voice at last!" And at this, unseen since the viewer was not switched on, the Maestro had scornfully smiled.

The concert was quite sold out. Beyond even the capacity of the concert stadium. Herds had paid, therefore, also to *stand* and listen in the gardens outside, where huge screens and vocaliani were to be rigged. It was to be a night of nights, the Night of the Mermaid. And after that night? Well.

She was a doll. A toy. An aberration and a game–which he had played and won.

One night for her, then, the best night of her little wooden life. That would be enough. Live her dream. Who should aim at more?

The venue for the concert was two miles inland of the city and the Laguna, up in the hills. This stadium was modern, a curious sounding-board of glazing, its supporting masonry embedded with acoustic speakers. The half-rings of seats hung gazing down to the hollow stage. They would be packed. Every place taken, the billionaire front rows to the craning upper roosts equipped with magnifying glasses. Amid the pines and cypresses outside, the huge screens clustered. Throughout the city too others would be peering at the Teleterra, watching, listening. And beyond the Laguna, the city, in many other regions all across the teeming and disassembled self-absorption of the planet, they too, whoever was able and had a mind to, they too glued to the relay of this performance.

Unusually the concert was to begin rather early, the nineteenth hour of that light-enduring mechanically-extended summer night. Sunset would commence just before twenty-one. And the dusk, prolonged by aerial gadgets, would last nearly until the twenty-second hour.

Almost everyone had learned about the new and special instrument–though not its nature. A *mermaid*? They could barely wait. Speculation had been rife in the media for weeks.

So they entered the stadium. And when first they saw–*it*–during that vast in-gathering, startled curses and bouts of laughter ran round the hall. What *was* it? Was it hideous or divine, barbaric or obscene? Unplayable, how not? Some joke.

Eventually the illumination sank and the general noise changed to that wild ovation always given the Maestro Folscyvio. And out he came, impeccably clad, his lush dark hair and handsome face, his slender, strong hands, looking at least a third of a metre taller than he was due to his lean elegance, and the lifts in his shoes.

Hushing them benignly, he said only this, "Yes. As you

see. But you must *wait* to *hear*. And now, we begin."

From the nineteenth almost to the twentieth hour, just as, muted and channelled through the venue's glassy top the sun westered, Folscyvio performed at his full pitch of stunningly brilliant (and heartless) mastery.

As ever, the audience were stirred, shaken, opened out like fans–actual fans, not fanatics–gasping, weeping, tranced slaves caught in the blinding blitzkrieg of his glare; they slumped or sat rigid until the interval. And after it, fuelled by drink, legal drugs, and chat, they slunk back nearly bonelessly for another heavenly beating.

And Folscyvio played on, assisted by his little robot orchestra. He took to him a piano, a mandolino. But all the while, the mermaid doll stood upright on her green cushion, with her green tail, her green eyes, her *smallness*–dumb. Obscure and... waiting.

Some twenty minutes before twenty-one, the sunset swelled, then faded. The ghostly dusk ashed down. It was the Silver Hour, when the shadows fall. And tonight, here, it would *last* an hour.

The penultimate acts of the show were done. The orchestra stopped like a clock. Folscyvio put aside the mandolin. Then, stepping forward quite briskly, he gave the signal, and the mermaid was whirled upside-down–whereupon he seized her. And as the crowd faintly mooed in suspense he settled her, in a few well-practiced moves, her head upon his shoulder, the hair flowing down his back like a wing. He lifted the bow out of its sword-like sheath, which until then had been hidden in a cleverly-spun chiascuro.

Silences had occurred in history. The city knew silences. *This* silence however was thicker than amalgamating concrete. In a solid silver block it cased the concert hall.

Folscyvio played to them, within this case, the mermaid violin.

High and burningly sweet, the tone of the strings. Pelt-deep and throbbing with contralto darkness, the tone of the strings. A vibrato like lava under the earth, a supreme updraught like a flying nightingale. A bitter pulsing, amber. A platinum upper register that pierced–a needle– to conjure an inner note, some sound known only at the dawn of time, or at its ending. Consoling sorrow, aching agony of joy.

Never, never had they heard, nor anyone ever conceivably, such music. Even they could not miss it. Even he–even Folscyvio–could not.

He had not mastered the instrument. *It* had mastered *him*. *It* played *him*. And somehow, far within the clotted blindness and deafness of his costive ego–he *knew*. The Maestro, mastered.

Perhaps he had dubiously guessed when practising, when planning out this ultimate scene upon his rostrum of pride.

Or perhaps even, at that watershed, he had managed to conceal the facts from himself. For truth did not always set men free. Truth could imprison, too. Truth could kill.

On and on. Passing from one perfect piece to the next, seamless as cloth-of-Paradise, Folscyvio the faultless instrument, and the violin played him. All through that Silver Hour. Until the shadows had closed together and not a mote of light was left, except where he still poised, the violin gleaming in his grip, the bow fluttering and swooping, a bird of prey, a descending angel.

But all-light melted away and all-quiet came back. The recital was over.

How empty, that place. As though the world had sunk below the horizon as already the sun's orb had done.

The artificial lights returned like fireflies.

There he stood, straight and motionless, frowning as if he did not, for a second or so, grasp where he was, let alone where he had been during the previous hour.

But the audience, trained and dutiful, stumbled to its feet. And then, as if recollecting what *must* come next, began to screech and bellow applause, stamping, hurling jewels down on to the stage. (It had happened before. Folscyvio had even, in the past, graciously kept some of them; the more valuable ones.)

After the bliss of the music, this acclaiming sound was quite disgusting. A stampede of trampling, trumpeting things–that had glimpsed the Infinite, and could neither make head nor tail of it, nor see what should be done to honour it.

Seemingly unceasing, this crescendo. Until it wore itself out upon itself. The hands scalded from clapping, the voices cracked with over-use. Back into their seats they crumbled, abruptly old, even the youngest among them. Drained. Mistaken. Baffled.

Inevitably, afterwards, there would be talk of a drug–illegal and pernicious–infiltrated into the stadium, affecting everyone there. But that rumour was for later, blown in like a dead leaf on the dying sigh of a hurricane.

Probably Folscyvio did suspect he was not quite himself. Some minor ailment, perhaps. A virus, flimsy and unimportant. Nevertheless he felt irritated, dissatisfied, although realising he had played superbly. But then, he always did. Nothing had changed.

Now he would swiftly draw this spectacle to a close. And in the favourite way: theirs. *His.*

He said, very coldly, (was he aware how cold?) "We will finish."

No one anymore made a noise. Sobered and puzzled, they hung there before him, all their ridiculous tiers of plush seats, like bits of rubbish, he thought, piled up in rows along gilded and curving shelves, in the Godforsaken fucking cupboard of this mindless arena.

He must have hesitated a fraction too long.

Then, only then, a scatter of feeble voices called out for the auction.

Folscyvio smiled, 'wintry and fastidious' as it was later described by an hysterical critic. "No. We will not bother with the *auction*. Not tonight. Fate is already decided. We will go directly to the sacrifice." For once some of them–a handful among the masses there–set up loud howls for mercy. But he was adamantine, not even looking towards them. When the wailing left off, he said, "She has had her night. That is enough. Who should aim for more?"

And after this, knowing the cue, the stadium operatives crushed the lights down to a repulsive redness. And on to the stage ran the automatic trolley which, when all this had begun those years ago, had been designed for the Maestro by his subordinates.

Again, afterwards, so much would be recalled, accurately or incorrectly, of what came next. All was examined minutely.

But it did no good, of course,

They had, the bulk of this audience, witnessed 'The Sacrifice' before. The sacrifice, if unfailingly previously coming *after* an auction, when invariably the majority of the crowd bayed for death, and put in bids for it, (the cash from which Folscyvio would later accommodate), was well known. It had been detailed endlessly in journals, on electronic sites, in poems, paintings and recreated photo-imagery. Even those who had never attended a Folscyvio concert, let alone a sacrifice, *knew* the method, its execution and inevitable result. The Maestro burned his instruments. Sometimes after years of service. Now and then as on this night, following a single performance.

Pianos and chitarras, such larger pieces, would tend to sing, to shriek, to call out in apparent voices, and to *drum* like exploding hearts in the torment of the fires. But the viosirenalino–what sound could she make, that miniature Thing, that doll-mermaid of glass, enamel and burnished wood and hair?

Despite everything, many of them were on the seats' edges to find out.

She leaned now, again upright in the supporting rays of

the magnetic beams. When he poured the gasoline, like a rare and treacly wine, in a broad circle all about her, saturating the green cushion, but not splashing her once, a sort of rumbling rose in the auditorium. Then died away.

Folscyvio moved back to a prudent distance. He looked steadily at the mermaid violin, and offered to her a solitary mockery of a salute. And struck the tinder-trigger on the elongate metal match.

Without a doubt there was a flaw in the apparatus. Either that, or some jealous villain had rigged the heavily security-provided podium. Or else–could it be–too fast somehow for any of them to work out what he did–did *he*, Folscyvio, somehow reverse the action? As if, maybe, perceiving that never in his life after that hour would he play again in that way, like a god, he wished to vacate the stage forever.

The flame burst out like a crimson ribbon from the end of the mechanical match. But the mermaid violin did not catch fire. No, no. It was Folscyvio who did that. Up in a tower of gold and scarlet, blue and black, taller even than he had been–or seemed–when alive, the Maestro flared, and was lost at once to view. He gave no sound either, as perhaps the violin would not have done. Was there just no space for him to scream?

Or was it that, being himself very small, and cramped and hollow and empty, there was no proper crying possible to him?

In a litter of streaming and luminous instants he was obliterated, to dust, a shatter of black bones, a column of stinking smoke. And yet–had any been able to see it?–last of all to be incinerated were his eyes. Narrow, long-lashed, grey-mauve, and–for the final and first time in Folscyvio's existence–full of fire.

Mills

A House on Fire

Edwin Marsh Onslowe strangled his mistress, Mrs. Violet North, in the early February of 1885. In order to conceal the crime, he then set a fire in her otherwise unoccupied and remotely situated house, which accordingly burned to the ground during the night. As their illicit affair had been scrupulously hidden by both parties, Onslowe was not even suspected of having anything to do either with the fire itself, or with the demise of Mrs. North. The latter was in fact judged carelessly and accidentally to have burned to death. Sometime later, however, Edwin Onslowe presented himself at a police station and freely confessed to arson and murder. He was subsequently found guilty and hanged.

The reason he gave for his confession has, ever since, remained the subject for perplexed debate.

—Derwent's Legal Mysteries

he heat of the fire on his face—
It was burning. *Burning....*

Travelling up on the train through a fading afternoon into the first encroachment of dusk, he was a little excited. More at the element of adventure, of course, than at seeing Violet again. She was hardly any longer a novelty.

In fact they had met five years before, and from the very start had carried on their rather intermittent affair in just this way, which was that of *subterfuge.* It had been for her sake. A married woman with a great amount to lose, she had had to be persuaded, or to persuade herself. Besides, their earliest meetings took place in spying, gossipy London, in a succession of small hotels somewhere between The Strand and the Hibernian Road.

To each of these they went separately, meeting near the agreed venue, pretending thereafter to be a married couple bound for Charing Cross Station and the boat train, and having to break an arduous journey in order to rest for three or four hours. Edwin, this scenario in mind, would always arrive with a pair of spurious bags–the other luggage having "already gone on ahead." No doubt that would have been quite enough to sustain their ploy. They were never challenged, treated with unsuspicious courtesy, and served tea at the end of their sessions. However, Edwin had instantly enhanced the little play.

Both he and she were to dress in modest clothes rather unlike their generally more elegant garments (for Violet, through her legal husband was rich, and Edwin, if hardly wealthy, still quite well off). Edwin, too, might employ a wig, even a false moustache. These he would apply, and later slough, in some convenient if chancy doorway or alley found en route. They would, each of them, talk in less polished accents and more hackneyed terms, as befitted apparel and hotel.

They would keep this up from the moment of publicly meeting until the bedroom door closed fast on their supposed siesta. Which was, evidently, the exact opposite of restful. Emerging after, they would continue their roles, mildly genteel little nobodies, until they parted, then without any visible sign of affection or even of ever having known each other, somewhere in the warren of streets.

Violet herself seemed to enjoy their game. Sometimes she would, once inside the hotel bedroom, dissolve in laughter, muffled initially by his hand, and then his eager mouth.

Certainly to begin with, Edwin was ardent, enticed by Violet's body–she was then just twenty-one years of age. But over the succeeding half-decade he must admit their liaison sank, for him at least, to a habit–one he might not much miss if given up. Nevertheless, the "game" *always* amused him.

He was playing it, naturally, when he journeyed out of London on the train. He sat in a second-class carriage, not overly full at that time of day or year, and watched the thick smoke and steam of passage drift by, and the wildlands of the more southerly northwest come and go between, in gathering afternoon, sunset and dusk. He was attired as a poorish office clerk, who liked to go walking in the country should he get a vacation. The inn he meant to stay at, too, just outside Pressingbury, was precisely the sort such a person would choose. Edwin had gone to some pains, as ever in his Violet episodes. But this, admittedly, had been a more complex project, made necessary by her having taken possession of some big old country house.

Violet had sent him a short letter, addressing him by the invented name of Mr. *Harbold*. She was newly in the house, and would he not come up in February. Then they could discuss the "important business" at hand.

Edwin, accepting the invitation with slight, if not completely tepid interest, had no notion what the "business" was, if indeed it were anything more than another code in their game. The faint irksomeness of the trip was offset for him by playing once more in disguise. He would stay tonight at the inn, then go off on his "little walking tour." The second day and night he would spend with Violet, returning from her new house directly to the town, and thence to London.

Violet's husband, Henry Augustus North, was at this time in India. More than fifteen years her senior, he had been there now almost a quarter of a century, in a mercantile rather than a military capacity. Now and then, of course, he was in England, as he had been when first they met. But now, as then, he never stayed long. The climate of England did not agree with North. Just as, Violet had convinced him, that of India, even untried, would never agree with *her*.

Edwin left the train at Pressingbury Halt. By then he was tired and hungry, buoyed up only by his disguise (he now was Mr. Harbold) and the play he would carry on at the inn to safeguard Violet's reputation. He walked the two miles to his lodging as twilight closed on the landscape. Edwin paid no attention to the beauty of the scenery, the steep boulderings of hills changing to the black furred backs of giant beasts, the eerie sparkle of a white waterfall, the glittering litter of the cool late-winter stars. It would be a longer walk tomorrow to the isolated property. And Violet would be demanding. (Rather like her husband, Edwin had not seen her for several months.) As he reached the inn and traipsed inside, Edwin did wonder, briefly, if tomorrow's might be, after all, the last time he spent with her.

As it happened, he had met a young woman only the week before, at the races. Iris Smithys was less high up the social ladder than Violet North, but only nineteen, with perfect figure, unmarked skin, and dancing eyes full of a sudden heat when they had met his own. Yes, truly, this might well be the last occasion he and Violet played any of their little games. They must, both, then, make the most of it.

"Edwin–my very dear–! How wonderful that you've arrived!"

She had grown old. In less than seven months her summer had been shed from her. Her flesh seemed dry, to see, to touch… No, this was absurd. She was not yet twenty-seven… Unless, as sometimes the female sex did, she had *lied.*

"Violet. More lovely than ever," he murmured, holding her close in the clandestine hallway.

"Alas no, my dearest. I'm not at my best, I know. It's been a troubling while. I wanted not to bother you with any of it until I had some knowledge of where I stood."

Alarm took a grip on Edwin, replacing the annoyed repulsion he had felt on viewing her drabness.

In spite of all Edwin's care–had old North discovered the adultery? Was he perhaps even now storming towards England across the ocean, polishing a pistol as he prowled the decks?

Her reply rushed the blood from Edwin's cheeks.

"We are to be divorced," said Violet, and burst into such a torrent of tears, it was as if a fountain had been turned on inside her eyes.

Edwin clamped himself in iron control.

"Are you in any danger, Violet?" He meant, naturally: Am I in any danger?

To his bemused relief she shook her head. "No, no–my very dear... Oh Edwin, it's been such a dreadful strain–yet now, perhaps, at last, something wonderful may come from it!"

Edwin was in several minds on this, but he followed Violet meekly into a large morning room that led off the hallway. He had seen no servants either within or without the house, and when presently Violet informed him she had dismissed them all for three days of holiday, he was unsurprised if perturbed. Obviously, to keep even the most trusted and loyal retainer on the premises during Edwin's sojourn would be unwise. But how, servantless, they were to manage he partly dreaded. He thought she would have no culinary skills beyond the making of a pot of tea, or the peeling of an apple.

But Violet was all enthusiasm. She ushered him to a chair and brought him, on a tiny tray, a glass of sherry and a plate of biscuits, with the oddly jaunty air of a silly child acting. Even so, her gloom seemed abruptly to have left her. She looked in the firelight (had *she* lit the fire?), softer and less unappealing as her face relaxed. "You see," she said, sitting on a stool at his feet, "this may come to be the best thing in the world, my love."

Gravely Edwin waited. "Yes?"

It was then, for the very first, the house made its presence known to him.

Edwin, as noted, was–despite his earnest game-playing–not especially observant, and particularly not of anything that was not *animate.* That is, a human being might attract his attention, either for some extreme of conduct, fair or foul, or likewise physical appearance. Even a dog or horse, or large bird, might also gain his regard, if sufficiently aggravating, smelly or threatening. The earth, however, unless in quake or eruption, could never do so. Not even the sea itself, unless he had been on it in the midst of a storm, something that so far he had sedulously avoided. The world was only shapes, lights and shadows, weather, and potential stupid accidents and assaults such as pitfalls or rabid sheep. Meanwhile all static objects, which must necessarily include the architecture of any building, whether a temple of the ancient Greeks, a pyramid of the uncanny Egyptians, or a slum behind a stable (rather resembling the place he had grown up in before a legacy came his way) had less impact on him than music on a stone.

He had had today a *very* long walk to reach his destination, aided only by Violet's badly drawn map. Therefore, this big and rangy house perched on the top of a hill, surrounded by rough if private woodland, and with a strange tall rectangular facade, had left him, until that moment in the morning room, entirely untouched.

The more curious then, maybe, the reaction that swept stilly yet intensely into and through him.

So powerful was the impression, although utterly

unnameable and nearly untranslatable, that for a second or so he failed to hear his mistress's twitterings.

If he had *had* to name it, *identify* it, as, rather later indeed he would struggle to do, he would say, *did* say, that he felt the house did not *like* him. Ridiculous though this was, it was the furthest he could get towards the root of the feeling. It did not *like,* nor did it *trust* him. And far, far worse than any prying servant, it seemed–through its hundreds of corners, its thousands of boards and cornices and angles, its countless ranks of windows–to be *watching* him with a terrible and immutable *attention.*

"Forgive me, Violet. This is a fine sherry–my thought was distracted for an instant. What did you say?"

"Oh, my dearest Edwin, I know it must all be such a startlement! Perhaps I should wait awhile. We can discuss everything after luncheon. I am so glad–so very glad you're here at last!"

Needless to relate, rather than discuss anything at all, they took the habitual "siesta" after lunch.

Edwin, who had not looked forward to this, now learned that some of the very good, if cold, food left by the vacant cook had cheered him, as had the wine. And in the dim curtained bedchamber on an upper floor, he found that, instead of comparing Violet with Iris Smithys, he was enabled to *conjure* Iris into and over Violet's willing, yearning flesh. He did not, then, fail to enjoy the afternoon. As for Violet, she was almost religious in her worship. Good God. She loved him. He had never fully accepted such a foible in her before. At the hour it added gloss. Then quite quickly it began to make him uneasy. And this was when, taking post-carnal tea as they had been used to do in the hotels, he felt again the "eyes" of the house upon him. Its ears were *listening.* The house was "weighing him in the balance," he was afterwards to declare. And the *house* had fathomed him as the idiotic Violet never had, or surely could. As even *he,* probably, had not.

Finally, when evening drew on, they sat in a big dark parlour inadequately lit by oil lamps (no gas, let alone electricity, had been brought to the house). And here Violet explained all that had recently occurred between her and Henry Augustus North, its impending events and ultimately seemingly unavoidable outcome.

North himself, the old duffer, had fallen in love not only with the Indian climate, but with some native woman, some alleged princess or *Rani*–or some such peculiar title. For her he had given up the Christian faith, and was now proposing to marry her. To this end he would allow Violet to divorce him, so no scandal should attach to her. The Rani was also, it transpired, well-to-do. North accordingly gave over a great many funds, shares, estates, and general interests to his soon-to-be-former wife. These things included the old house in the hills.

Violet said she had been calamitously upset by all of this; it seemed she must have reckoned him mostly faithful, even if *she* were not. She had felt, she announced, shamed, abandoned, scorned, and ruined. Yet, on coming to the house, she had fallen in love (oh, love again) with it immediately. It was a domicile, she told Edwin, said to have inherent healing qualities. For example, some male ancestor of the present Mr. North, during the previous century, had been miraculously cured here of a loathsome disease, while any woman brought to bed with child on the premises delivered a hale and fortunate baby, and herself suffered no harm.

Such stories normally contemptuously tickled Edwin. Now he frowned. But Violet went on, expatiating at enormous length, with the exuberance if not the flare of a professional storyteller, on the house's mystical pre-history. How the ground, the hill and its woods, were formerly some blessed site in "times of yore," how all the bricks and stones, beams, even cements and joists that glued and stitched the place together, had been taken from marvellous and legendary areas, not merely in England, but over all Europe–a type of wood from some sacred antique forest, a rare marble said to have been created from ice and the blood of a saint. More than this, during the erection of the house, which, the tale had it, went on about the middle of the 1600s, not only planners and architects but every mason, carpenter and artisan of any sort was tested, and proved to be pure in heart and intellect before he took a part in the building.

Perhaps, at another season, Edwin, here, might politely have stifled a yawn. Now he was deluged by a unique and almost horrified irritation. Like the yawn, he held it in. And eventually Violet reached her conclusion. This involved her statement that, in the end, she had come to understand her husband's latent and luminous kindness to her in his giving of the house. She had, since being here, also recovered much of her general vitality, and hoped for a complete renewal. For these reasons she had finally sent for Edwin.

"You bloom, dear Violet," he drawled, and sipped the glass of champagne, whose bottle he had had to open.

"Yes, Edwin, I'm better, and will be better still–" (For her sake he hoped so.) "But, in addition, do you see what a chance we have now–that is, once the divorce is settled?"

Distracted by the scrutiny of shadows and silences, drained by false lovemaking, rather, he must admit, *on edge,* Edwin stared at her. He had no idea what Violet meant. He should not have been so slow. But never mind it, next moment, with a glowing smile, she was to enlighten him.

"Edwin, you and I–we can at last be absolved of any guilt, and rescued from our lonely longing. We can marry, Edwin. I can be your wife! No stigma can connect to me. And I shall be wealthy now in my own right. We shall be rich, Edwin! And–my own beloved–we shall be *one,* as surely God has always meant us to be."

Dinner was cold as well. He found now it did not cheer him

so much, not even with the excellent Burgundy, and purplish port, not even the imported and splendid cigars she had contrived to get him.

He saw, too, her eyes beginning to gleam once more with the renewal of lust. He had managed that earlier, but again? Edwin thought not.

He began to make his excuses. They were sufficiently feeble. He seemed, he said, to have caught a chill during his walk to the house; he was not well. And it had been something of a shock, her news, he must admit. He had been so concerned for her…

Oh, women. Such fools, but so sharp always when their primal needs went unmet, so *clever,* with the base intelligence of some lower animal–Violet had sussed him out instantly. Her eyes burst forth their tears once more. Did he not want her? But they could be married–all her considerable money should be his. Did he not *love* her? She had always thought he did. Why else–*how* else–had he persuaded her to dishonour, dragged her into wicked adultery. She loved *him.* He was her world.

"Violet, you misread me now," he blurted, frightened of her feral urgency. The most civilised of females, he had long known, could turn in a second from Belle to Beast. "I'm not myself this evening. I must go to bed, forgive me. We can talk again tomorrow." And he rose, male authority pulled about him like a steely mantle. Violet responded with inertia. As sometimes even the most hysterical of women did. They had been so dominated, commanded, almost from the cradle. It was God's law. Man was king. "Tomorrow," he frigidly promised, slinking out of the door. "We will discuss all this then." He did not risk a perhaps consoling paternal kiss on her forehead. Through her flood of tears, he saw the flames of crucifying truth burning her up, like a narrow pale house on fire within, the casements splintering at the heat, and the scarlet and gold of arson blazing from its riven skull.

Out in the passage, where the candlelight was thin and

isolated, Edwin Marsh Onslowe felt the weirdest throb, a sort of non-physical lurch, crunch through the building. It was, it went without saying, only the differentiation of the cold night beyond the walls and the internal warmth of lamps and fires, metal and wood expanding, contracting. Such things were not supernormal.

With luck, she would weep herself to sleep, and at first light he could, in the nondescript disguise of clerkly Mr. Harbold, quit the unsettling house, and the awful company of Violet North, forever.

It was not to be. Certain matters, it seemed, were already, as the Eastern poets said, written in some momentous book.

Notwithstanding the prologue, he was tired, and sleep came swiftly. He had no dreams he recalled. Yet his slumber was fretted by a kind of half-conscious anxiety–the premonition of Violet's revenge–traducing him, filthying his name, of hiring men to murder him even, or, oddly worse, somehow forcing him, despite everything, to marry her, and so decay beside her for fifty years of dreary hell.

In actuality, Violet stole, about three in the morning, into the separate bedroom prepared for him, a room (clearly) she had not expected him to select.

Asleep, he woke in panic as she flung herself upon him, her flailing weight, her burning hot skin, and tear-melted eyes, screaming and sobbing out all those emotions she had, until that minute, so stringently clamped for twenty-seven years in the prison of her heart.

The fear he felt was colossal. Probably it made his excuse.

As before, when she had sometimes giggled so loudly and insanely in those hotel bedrooms, or indeed in other stages of their passion when she grew too noisy, he clapped his right hand over her mouth. In the past, he would have kissed her next. Not now. Exerting another strength he had, which perhaps he could never have foreseen he might possess, left-handed he seized her throat. At which his right hand let go of her face and flew to join its partner. Grasping her neck in both hands (that seemed to him in those moments incredibly large, too large to belong to him) he did not merely choke the life from her, but snapped the bones of her upper spine free of her skull, as if they had only been the slender stems of glass goblets.

When Edwin had finished killing Violet, he did another–to himself, later–astonishing thing. He rolled her body straight off the bed onto the floor. There it lay then, in its coil of nightgown and robe, for the rest of the hours of darkness, while he slept in a deep and dreamless stupor on his back, at the centre of the mattress.

The commencement of dawn light on the ceiling woke him. It was rosy, one of those icing-sugar winter dawns often shown on picture cards of happy skaters, or small animals frolicking in wintry woods. Edwin lay, slightly confused, staring up at it, thinking it first the reflection of his fire, but the fire in the grate was out, naturally. He could not, for a little while, recollect where he was. Then he remembered he was in Violet's country house. And then he remembered all of it.

He sat up very slowly, and in a shrinking terror looked down over the side of the bed to the bundle of washing and loose hair on the carpet. Then he buried his head in his hands and wept in despair. Rather as Violet had done, but Edwin did not really think of that.

In the greater part of humankind there resides an instinct for survival. It is this which can clutch at straws and effect a rescue from them. It is this which can, now and then, outwit fate.

After some time Edwin, as he believed, pulled himself together and got up. Having dressed, he went down through the house to the kitchens, where he soon located some cold beef, a loaf, and butter. Since tea and coffee had not been made, of course, he did not bother with them but charged himself with a brandy and soda in the drawing room.

In the new day–a bluish but very cold one, with frost visible on the windows, and on the edges of boughs and walls–the house, with its unlit hearths, looked quite deadly to him. Although, as has been said, Edwin lacked imaginative perception, he felt the hollowness of the place, as if it, too, were frozen both out and in. But this fancy was one he did not dwell on. He had by now mastered himself. He had done something shocking and harsh, even if driven to it by extreme provocation. He doubted any man alive, unless an uplifted priest or a fool, could have done otherwise. It seemed almost as if she–Violet–had given herself to him as a sacrifice. But again, such a notion was not to be considered now. For Edwin must make a plan.

The excellent and rejuvenating fact was that, as he had come here in his disguise of the humble, irrelevant Harbold, *Edwin* had had no role in any subsequent event. Nor could he be suspected of having one. Nobody at all had ever known of Edwin's connection with Violet North. While, and in this he did trust her fully, Violet would never have betrayed her relationship with him. She had always been far too afraid of losing her husband, or more properly, the financial parasol North had maintained over her head. As for the invented Harbold himself, even he had evidenced no link with Violet. He had gone off on his doltish country walk, vanishing from the inn, a dull little nobody soon forgotten.

It only remained, therefore, for Edwin to go home–if perhaps now in a slightly altered disguise. This posed no difficulty. He had always taken a few spare articles of dress with him, even a secondary wig, on his jaunts with Violet; it was, for him, part of the fun. And in this manner, *Harbold* need not be seen again *anywhere*. While Edwin must have been in London all the time, at his quiet lodging, immersed in his own harmless projects.

Edwin went to change his clothes and don the other wig, which was a rather nicer one than he had given poor Harbold. That done, Edwin went very carefully over the house, and through each room he had, however briefly, occupied. In the process of doing this, inevitably, he came upon Violet's body again, still laid out like rolled-up washing beside the bed. Edwin was by then completely in control of himself. So much so in fact that he thought her very unseemly. Caught by a curious whim, he had half an urge to move the corpse, to stuff it possibly into its own bed, but he sternly resisted such childishness. Instead he returned alone to the master bedroom, where Violet and he had spent the previous afternoon. Here he paused, brooding.

Of course, it could not be denied, there was *every* evidence *here* that the woman had been with a lover. Scowling, Edwin took in various signs he was too fastidious to name to himself–they had been careless here, as not in the cheap hotels. And she had troubled to tidy nothing. It was a pity, he thought then, with admirable practicality, he had not killed her before any of *that* took place. Could there be clues here after all that might, despite all odds, reveal his actions?

Just then the house gave off a massive cracking creak. It must remind any who had ever heard such a noise of the snapping of bones.

Edwin's nerve, for a fragment of a second, also snapped. He shouted at the house. "It's the damned cold! Just the cold makes such a sound in you! You need a bloody fire to warm you up."

Epiphanies are often bizarre, and come in many forms.

That which came to Edwin caused him physically to stagger. But then he stood in utter silence, staring about him, his hands already flexing, his mind already racing. And the house, too, the house was entirely silent. Silent as the grave.

Setting the fire was very easy. Her unmodern residence was full of candles, tapers, matches, lamps, and oil. Edwin went about his task quite methodically, but also with a certain exhilaration. He could not hide from himself that he nearly relished this ultimate act of cleansing, after all the foolish mess Violet had made for him. He understood he did her also a great service. No opprobrium now could ever attach itself to her character.

So thorough Edwin was (and so sensible, pausing even to partake of a quick luncheon in order to keep up concentration and stamina), that the sun was low when, his own luggage safely out on the lawn, Edwin struck and scattered the first of his incendiaries.

He presently beat a hasty retreat, for the fire obligingly took hold everywhere, and with a slightly surprising efficiency. But then, he had been immaculate. He had made a proper job of it. What bewilderment the returning servants would receive, he vaguely thought, when he had got himself off along the drive and down onto the wooded slopes of the hill. By then he could smell the tang of smoke out in the fresh cold of a darkling dusk. Turning at length, he looked back, and saw to his immense relief and satisfaction an unearthly glow and flicker–rather like, conceivably, that of the northern lights–going on in the upper air above the trees. Then, even as he gazed transfixed, there came a huge, wide *bang*, like thunder, and through the twilight overhead darted an explosion of spangling elements, as if insects burst from some shell.

A cinder dashed on Edwin's cheek, a miniscule scorch sharp as a tiny sting. At this, it occurred to him that, with luck, even the old trees on the hillside might very well also go up in smoke. Wisely then he ran, his bag clutched tight, and the downhill path quite helpful now he was past the larger tree roots, and soon well lighted by the burning house behind.

Not until he had reached flatter ground, due to make southwards now along deserted country tracks, did Edwin permit himself one further viewing of his masterpiece.

By that time all he could make out was a vast black cloud rising hundreds of feet into the sky, that let out of itself quite regular bright fountains, and through which occasionally some dull crimson shape evolved, more like a noise than a sight, a sort of *roar,* a soundless *bellowing.*

It was a wearisome plod on foot and without detour to the station. But from there a late train took him to the town of Pressingbury. He could, in his smarter character, stay tonight at the Pressingbury Arms. Tomorrow there remained only the uneventful journey to London, and a little well-deserved peace.

Some seven days later, rested and recovered, Edwin Onslowe invited Iris Smithys to accompany him to the seaside, since the weather in the south-east had become clement. She consented and they visited the pier at Hastings, resplendent with its Eastern Pavilion. Iris flirted deliciously with Edwin all morning, and ate a fish luncheon with him, but declined a mutual spell in one of the more attractive hotel bedrooms.

This angered Edwin. He felt, perhaps correctly, Iris had strung him along. They returned to London in sullen non-communication.

Truth to tell, once parted from the girl, he was rather reluctant to go back to his flat on Tenmouth Street, behind the Temple. He passed a further hour or so at a public house, but found the pub fire far too hot. It had been a very mild day.

The heat of the fire on his face. It was burning, drying his skin so that his flesh seemed to stick to his bones. His hot eyes filled with water...

Rising cursing from this dream, the first dream he had fully recalled for months, Edwin opened the window of his bedroom and peered into the street below. Gas-lamps blurred and flickered. But even in the fresher air he could smell the poisons of the room's blocked chimney. He must speak to the bloody landlord again. God knew, he paid enough rent.

Quite often Edwin indulged in buying all the reputable newspapers, and reading them at home. He had accordingly done this for three consecutive days, and so found, on the evening of the third, several references to a dramatic rural house fire. In the item Violet was still, very properly, spoken of as Mrs. Henry North, and a brief comment made on the tragedy of her comparative youth and the likelihood that, the body's having been found in the bedroom, she had wakened too late to fly. Most likely also the blaze was caused, the more proselytising journal added, by careless use of an unguarded flame. It added a paragraph on the very severe danger of leaving lit candles in passages, or banked fires burning overnight.

Though icy, the week had been very dry, and both the house and much of the surrounding and ancient woodland were consumed. Violet herself, as Edwin learned from a more scurrilous rag the next day, had been fairly consumed, her corpse only identifiable by a remnant of her wedding ring, which was composed of white silver rather than gold.

Edwin Onslowe found himself cool throughout his reading of these facts. He had kept his head, and would continue to do so. Sometimes, it was true, he did feel slightly sorry for her, if only for a moment. Then he recalled how upset she had been on learning he did not love or wish to marry her. Her life thereafter would only have been a misery to her. Really, she had made a lucky escape.

On the evening of the fifth day Edwin dined at his club in Bleecher Street. Coming back about eleven-thirty at night he found, on entering his flat, that a rank smell of smoke hung around it. He, despite the paper's warning, had as ever left a fire in the apartment, albeit safely caged behind the fireguard. Edwin concluded something had happened in the chimney, and promptly descended the house to wake his landlord. As a rule, landlord and tenants did not have direct dealings, and the nightshirted gentleman was not best pleased to meet with Edwin at a quarter to midnight. However, it was arranged that the chimney should be investigated on the morrow.

The next day then was occupied throughout by a visitation of sweeps and similar mechanicals. The chimney was swept and pronounced in order, and other appliances vindicated of blame.

Worn out by this tiresomeness, yet somewhat looking forward to *the following* day (on which he was to escort Miss Smithys to Hastings), Edwin had that night dropped into a heavy sleep.

After the Hastings trip, Iris' aggravating behaviour, and the odd dreams of burning heat, Edwin woke rather later than usual, about nine, and getting up, could still smell, as in the night, horribly strong and fetid smoke in every room of the apartment. Once more the landlord was summoned, and the man having this time ungraciously climbed the four flights, declared there was no smell at all.

"Well, I've been forced to open all the windows. Fortunately the weather's mild, or I'd no doubt have caught a chill."

"'Tisn't that mild," rejoined the landlord, scanning the frosted avenue below. "Maybe it's your nasal corridors that are at fault, Mr. Onslowe. When the wife takes cold she can smell smoke in her nose from the catarrh. Common phenomenon," he added loftily.

"I am not your damn–I am not your wife."

"Well," said the landlord, "I'd recommend you visit your physician, Mr. O. I'm not about to call out the sweep again when the chimneys aren't at fault." So saying he left.

Edwin soon also vacated the premises, needing, he felt, clean air. He would have to move, he decided, as he strode through the grasslands of Hyde Park, staring in disapproval at the feeding sheep. Some smaller apartment in some nicer venue, why not?

After luncheon Edwin returned to his rooms, and did notice an elusively smoky odour out on the street. A fog perhaps was building itself up from the puffing chimneys of thousands of homes and places of commerce. After all, from these alone there was a constant basic underflavour of smoke that, like the horse dung, one seldom noticed. Probably he had *imagined* the excess inside his flat. (Edwin evidently did not realise he had little imagination.) Nevertheless, on undoing his door he was assailed at once by a choking miasma so awful he began to retch. Inclined to rush out again, he yet rushed forward, alarmed that something was indeed burning. Nothing was. The room lay warm yet grey, the hearths all dead.

Only then did it come to him what the real cause of this "phenomenon" might be. And at the idea, his heart leapt and clutched at his breast. The clothes he had worn on the night of his departure from Violet's house, the very wig, the shoes, the bag itself–they remained in his wardrobe, and must be imbued by smoke. He had not considered the need do anything to or with them, save store them as before. Certainly, he had detected no telltale smell of cinders or burned material on them previously, not even in the hotel at Pressingbury, let alone on the London-bound train. Yet surely here lay the cause of the rancid and bitter stink. Shut up in the dark (like his crime, had he considered it), no doubt the staleness had intensified, and his nose, more acute than those of others, grew quickly aware.

These remnants of the "game" must go. Out, out of the flat, out of his life. He would dispose of them as soon as evening fell.

He did not don another disguise. He had told himself, quite strictly, such immature pursuits should cease. Even so, he waited until full darkness sank on the city. It was a dark that not even the gas street lighting, not even the blaring windows of shops and taverns could properly disperse. There was also, indeed, he believed, a hint of mist. It swirled about the corners of things, and breathed out from the mouths of passersby.

He took the bag and all its contents, which comprised both "costumes" from his visit to Violet, and walked along with casual briskness. He had not conceived a plan. Yet somehow it had been borne in on him that to follow the river a way might well be the best course. Tonight the tide was high. What could be more apt than to pause awhile, then let his burden fall. If any stray found it after, pulled down or upstream by the sea-tending Thames, it could mean little.

He noted idly as he went along, something slightly peculiar about the gas lamps. Even, now he gave attention, the occasional brazier at a street corner. The fires in both seemed oddly extended, and in some cases to be actually *fizzing*. They gave off, he felt, unnecessary heat. Someone should look into it.

Edwin came out on the fine, elongated terrace of the Embankment. It was a calm night, and down on the black serpent of the water, a fire-funnelled steamer and a couple of small tugs plied their passage. Edwin glanced at the Egyptian Obelisk, erected only a few years before, a silly folly he had always thought it. But now, something in the tall narrow *upwardness* of it momentarily unnerved him. From its topmost point a kind of glinting ray seemed intermittently to spark–some trick of the murky evening.

A few more persons passed him. Then came a stretch where no one was save he. All about, in the near distance, the busy metropolis galloped and hurried. But up against this artery of watery night he stood, for a space, alone. Edwin did as he had meant to. He leaned a little, the bag raised up by his chest. Below, straight down, beyond the stone steps, there expanded what looked like black liquid coal. A mile deep it seemed, but could not be. Deep enough.

Presently the bag dropped, noiseless, until it touched the surface with only the least audible of splashes. But then. Time felt as if it had stopped–or, not exactly stopped... time had *hesitated.* Edwin beheld the bag's conglomeration of falsehood and old smoke entering the river with the solid motion of a thing far heavier. And as the river took it, then closed again above it, out on the skin of the water a hundred brilliant golden eyes came crackling and buzzing. They were little fires, little dancing yellow flames, each with a coil of bluish smoke. In utter astonishment Edwin stared at them, as they budded and bubbled there, shining so bright. Until with a popping hiss, as one they all went out, leaving only a long, thick wreath of smoulder that filed slowly away between the gaps of the night.

During the next weeks, a pair of journals carried a reference to Mrs. North's burial somewhere on the Isle of Wight. A number also bore news that her husband, a merchant-trader then resident in India, had been suspected of arranging his wife's death, since he wished to marry elsewhere. However, without a shred of evidence he was soon cleared of all blame. By then a damp and sluggish February had lapsed into a rampaging, iron-clad March. Edwin Onslowe, it must be said, had given slight heed to either papers or weather. He had other matters on his mind.

The night after casting his bag of disguises into the Thames, with such an odd result, he had dined in the West End. The meal was overcooked, and while coming back, a thickening of the fog gave him a cough.

Back in his rooms he found the air no better, and once again inwardly determined to move. He slept badly, constantly waking up thinking he had heard a loud cracking noise, as if a large bough had broken from a tree. But no trees stood near his lodging. Getting up at first light, he saw the street again sugared by frost, and on touching the windowsill pulled off his hand with a cry. It would seem the surface was so cold it had felt scaldingly hot–a curious sensory error he had heard described, yet never formerly experienced. His fingers remained sore for half an hour.

That day he called on Iris Smithys, who permitted him to take her to luncheon. She would allow nothing else, and on parting, informed Edwin she would probably be unable to continue their "friendship," as another gentleman in her life had taken offense at it.

As Edwin marched back through the city, he was conscious of sweating with rage. And near St. Martin's, another unpleasant event befell him. One of those braziers with which London appeared then to be overstocked, let off a huge gout of sparks and red cinders just as he went by. Edwin, as if attacked by bees, leapt about in panic, beating out the fiery debris which had landed on his coat and in his hair, his hat on the pavement and his hands and face smeared with black. Rather than show concern, a nearby group of traders came closer to laugh at him. And when in fury he bawled profanities, he was accosted by the burliest and least wholesome of them, who manhandled Edwin, remarking, "Must be a bleedin' lunatic, you. Clear off, or I'll call the coppers." Edwin prudently went on his way.

In his flat he found many minute scorches on his face, a singed eyebrow, and tiny holes burned in his greatcoat. The scorches, even the singe, faded during the evening. The punctures in the coat also seemed to heal—some visual trick, no doubt, of the unreliable gaslight in his rooms, which had started to flicker distractedly and give out a strange resinous smell. He turned off the lights and resorted to candles. But these smoked, and were too hot to put up with.

He passed a wretched night, coughing and sweating so he feared he had a fever. And again he was frequently woken, from any brief sleep he had, by some noise, the source of which he could never locate, but that would seem to indicate a large rat in the attic, stumbling about and knocking the brickwork loose.

The *heat* of the fire on his face—

It was burning. *Burning*...

Why in God's name was he standing here, so near to this dangerously incendiary sight, however compelling? The tall house was almost by now engulfed in the vast tidal waves of the fire, the flames seeming of extraordinary size, as if made in some other world of giants, where even the elements must exist on a bigger scale. Out from the chimneys they poured in scarlet plumes, while the roofs ran like molten gold.

And behind him, all down the hill, the dry old woods had already caught, their winter boughs breaking into hot foliage, rose-red or yellow as the eyes of tigers. The sky even was like a dense amber dome.

He coughed ceaselessly. His lungs were tangled by the thick brown smoke. His eyes no longer ran with water, they bulged, and the moisture in them seemed to be boiling–he must at least shut his eyes, but he could not. And he could not turn and run.

A massive explosion, like a cannon shot, resounded from the house's core. Up through the cooking orange jam of air, the entire architecture seemed to rise. It did so with a weird, slow powerfulness. While off from every angle of it, the stones and bricks, the wood and marble and glass, went flying. One more deadly swarm. High, high the amalgam of chaos soared, then shattered and came spinning back towards the earth.

Already slabs and shards fell all around him, each detonating as it struck the ground. Oh, he must run away—he *must*...

Pleading, Edwin Onslowe woke in his London bed. He fought with his sheets, the blank dark night, his boiled eyes starting from his flame-roasted face.

And then he flopped down again with a pitiful mewing.

How long he lay thereafter, still coughing a little, the tears now unbottled and laving his parched skin, he never knew. *It was done. It was over.* So he told himself. *You simpleton, a dream. What else?*

How dark it was now. Were the street lamps even alight? Puzzled, reaching for normalcy, he made to rise. But in that moment a soft amorphous glow began. Edwin lay back. He had only thought the light was gone. Look, there it was, shining through the curtains and upward along the edges of the ceiling, a pale rosy light, like that from a low-burning hearth.

Perhaps three seconds it cheered him. Then he saw that in colour it was quite wrong, not to mention in strength. For see how it grew, and as it did the room filled with heat.

All his ceiling glowed now, a vivid restless red. And as through his curtain spiked an upsurge of light shafts like knives, he heard the loud blows and cracks above him of the blazing attics beginning to give way . . .

Edwin sprang from the bed, but did not reach even the window. A smothered dizziness, a stampede in his head–as unconsciousness axed him to the carpet, he knew he would lie there at the bedside, in his nightshirt resembling a roll of washing, until the flames had eaten all of him from the bone, and baked the bone to calcined and unidentifiable black.

The landlord demanded extra rent in lieu of proper notice. Edwin refused. "Count it," he coldly said, "your penalty for a rotten chimney and poorly maintained gas fitments."

Finding and securing another apartment had, of course, taken up a generous amount of March. Edwin had been meticulous, and wisely so. He did not mean to saddle himself with such a punishment twice.

No wonder he had had bad dreams in that vile place. No wonder his eyes sometimes flecked over with hosts of brilliant little sparkles (like sparks?), or darkened with cloudiness (rather like smoke, perhaps). This was all due to his upset nerves. The flat in Tenmouth Street was, he believed by then, a potential death trap. Not only the temperamental gas, and the reeking chimneys, but the water had started to run boiling hot from the vaunted "modern" faucets. Besides this, most of the surfaces in the rooms intermittently burned his hands. Once a *teacup* left hurtful, blood-red marks on palm and fingers for seventy minutes (he had timed the horror). Strangely, there were never blisters.

Inevitably, he continued to experience terrifying nightmares under such circumstances. He had convinced himself, however, as a rational man must, that no matter how real they seemed, they were only the result of so many petty, or alarming annoyances in the waking world. Even so, the nightmares affected his health. He felt always sweaty and feverish, and noted uneasily, with embarrassment, a faint rank charcoal odour lingering in his most newly laundered clothes, as if his own body by now emitted it. His hands, if not scorched by something, carried dirty smears that apparently spontaneously appeared on them–nonsense, naturally. Attending to his fingernails, black grit was often removed. When in other environs, aside from the fever, and the random visual disturbances, he seemed to think he was much better. Although it was a little odd, too, the number of small fires he noted everywhere–sometimes even reflections in puddles seeming startlingly to flame. Or sunset in some window, igniting, crackling, flashing... But there. He was under such strain.

The new apartment lay in rather a run-down street of Lambeth. There were fewer amenities, and the rooms were more cramped. But it boasted a fine view of a little public garden, and was, if anything, inclined to be draughty and cold, which he, always now so overheated, positively relished.

He was to move in on April 2. The night before, forced to sleep at Tenmouth Street, which sometimes lately he had avoided (putting up in a small hotel–he slept only in snatches but dreamed as a rule far less), Edwin dosed himself with a chemist's powder.

Whatever happened, tomorrow he would cross the river–cross running water–and be free of all this insanity.

Such a notion–the crossing of water–did not remind him that this exact gambit was used in popular fiction in order to elude a vengeful spirit.

Had he, recently, thought of Violet? Maybe he had, but if so only deep within his not yet fully recognised unconscious.

Steeped in the powder, he slept. But he thrashed and groaned, the drug altering his nightmares into a sort of burial by clinker and soot.

Morning arrived. Edwin drove himself to be sprightly. And the second day of April smiled upon him. Weak sun held off the rain. The removal van and reliable horse conducted those movables that were his away to Lambeth without a hitch. By the dinner hour, Edwin was installed, fussing with positions of chairs and tables as happily as some old lady with her ornaments. He did not care. Now all should be well.

He dreamed he was with Violet on the train to Hastings. He wished he were not, was bored and irritable. Until she suddenly vanished into thin air. Delighted, he took no issue with her disappearance. Next instant, others in the carriage were pointing out of the window at a burning edifice up on a tall hill.

All of them seemed frightened, and Edwin also grew afraid. Indeed, they were all well advised to be, for gradually, as the train ploughed on, the burning house came swelling down the hill after them, and, netted about with woods on fire and glass bursting like fireworks, ran on the track at their side.

All the other passengers then fled the carriage, but Edwin could not move, though the train windows grew ever hotter and melted like wax.

In the first of the most terrible earlier dreams Edwin had woken, or thought he had. That time, he thought he had tried to reach the window, but fainted. He certainly found himself next day lying by the bed.

Now, erupting from the dream of the train running neck and neck with the burning house, Edwin flung upright. Where was he? Tenmouth Street? No, no, he was shot of that place. Nevertheless, after all, even into Lambeth the nightmares had hunted him and pulled him down.

Edwin moaned. How impenetrably dark the room was. Of course, he had new curtains, very thick. No light could enter from the street.

He reached for matches, but had forgotten to put them by. He must get up and cross the room, turn on the gas above the mantelpiece ... or draw the curtain back an inch, perhaps.

A single unwary notion came to him as he swung his feet towards the floor. Was it Violet? Was it actually possible that Violet... haunted him? *Don't be a fool.*

The floor, lino rather than carpet, was cool to his feet. Thank God. And the blackness was without any smell, neither any sound. Oh, he would light a lamp, have a brandy, play a game of Patience. All would be well; he could not expect to slough all his trouble in a single evening.

As his hand touched the curtain, like the trick of a cheap but cunning magician, a thousand little golden embers winked on all over it. They twinkled and fluttered, scrambling up the folds. His eyes, it was only that; it would pass in a moment... Ignoring the illusion, even though it burned his hand, he dragged the heavy material aside. And there, directly below, instead of a street and a small garden, Edwin beheld the side of a craggy wildwood hill, sloping downwards into sheer darkness, under a starless sky. But even so, the stars were waking up. They were in the trees.

They were red and gold. They glittered and jostled, and long threads of purple vapour spiralled up from them. There came a sound like the hissing of snakes.

"No," Edwin said, with a nonsensical firmness, to the room, the night. But it was much too late for *No.*

The swarm of sparks came out from every direction, whirling at him, covering him, and by their solar flare, he saw his own hands beating at them, and in the round mirror opposite to him was the face of a madman shrieking...

Such a mirror had never been his. It was another mirror, that maybe he remembered. It had hung in that house.

By the naked flicker of sparks, of hurrying flames that skittered now everywhere, Edwin saw the cramped room had expanded to several times its size. Its ceiling had risen and was graced by cornices, and over there a solid beam–it was not the room in Lambeth, let alone in Tenmouth Street.

"A dream–!" shrilled Edwin.

The heat came in a torrent, a towering shout. For a scintillant second he could look straight through every wall. He saw the architecture of the huge old house, its narrow upright structure, the struts of stone or wood that pinned its brickwork, the tessellations of its roofs, the castle-shapes of chimneys, ziggurats of stairs, the weaving web of corridors and annexes, halls, and antechambers, the furniture that clad it, the drapes and papers and carpets that dressed it. He saw all this by the fiery torch of regnant flame, for the fire already gouged and conquered every avenue. The smell of smoke now was so acrid it had transmuted his lungs also to fire. He rushed from side to side, and slender vestiges of things floated or slammed towards him, gilded with their bright soprano pain.

Violet–he thought–*Violet.* But here, too, he was quite wrong. It was not Violet–poor, pathetic, tear-sodden ninny–not *she* he had brought inadvertently away with him from those two nights of homicide and arson. All about him now, crackling and cracking, timbers breaking, atoms raining down in lava showers, all about him screaming with its own speechless fury and despair, all about him was the vengeful ghost of what he, Edwin Marsh Onslowe, had also slain. Built on a site of blessing, constructed with care and talent from all that was benign, a healer, a protector. Replaying for him its endless dying agony. Of course, it was not any *human* psyche that had pursued him. It was the *ghost of the murdered house.*

The bedroom door, as Edwin wrenched it wide, burned the flesh from his hands. Howling, vomiting, he blundered through the ghastly radiance of passages, between the black bones of walls, and down its volcano-glass of blazing stairs. But there was no way out. Even had he found one, beyond the door, the gate, the land was burning too, its ancient trees, the very sky.

A hundred shattered mirrors showed him also how *he* had become. He was burned black, his facial bones a slate of scoria. He was so scalded that he shivered as if with icy cold. He, like the house, was quite dead, yet did not die. From his own mouth his unbreath issued out more flames. His boiled eyes bulged and glared. He did not know his name, he did not know himself.

Only what he had done. And that this, *this* would never end.

Edwin was discovered the next morning lying in an alleyway some five streets from his new apartment. He wore only his nightshirt, was both bruised and dirty, and some of his hair had been torn out.

The constable, who subsequently escorted him back to his lodging, confirmed that Edwin seemed to have received some dreadful shock, but he was by then subdued and decorous. He agreed to all the constable's requirements with a look of "almost relief." At the flat Edwin tidied himself and dressed. The two men then went by cab to the nearest police station.

Regardless of the fact that Edwin Onslowe's reason for admitting to the murder of Violet North, perhaps understandably, was never credited, his concise outline of his acts and motives convinced the arbitrators of the law. Guilt, meanwhile, as is well known, may assume varied aspects. Onslowe himself is said to have stated that, since his arrest, the remorseless haunt, or as others took it to be, nightmare, had donned a less awful if still persistent form, which involved mostly his watching, from outside, the house burn down. To Mrs. North herself, Onslowe never referred with any interest, let alone display of regret.

One further anecdote, conceivably, is worth noting.

Prior to his execution, Onslowe spoke with the priest, then customary. But Onslowe is reported to have told this gentleman immediately: "I neither hope for, nor fear, anything in any life after death. Following death there is nothing at all. For if there were another life, why do ghosts remain to trouble us in this one? My Hell I've suffered. Once dead, my dear sir, I expect–confound it–to get some peace."

—Derwent's Legal Mysteries

Eva, Beneath the Serpent Tree

Eva, beneath the Serpent Tree,
Was combing her sulphurous hair
With a comb made out of an elephant's tooth,
While she sat in a cedar-wood chair.

Her tresses were dyed by the sap of a plant,
(Crushed in a mortar of bone
Which had come from a large whale harpooned in the North), This imparted their daffodil tone.

Her dress it was sewn from the skin of a shark,
And trimmed with the elegant fur
Of young seals' coats which, her friends had remarked,
Looked more to advantage on her.

Oysters had died by barrel-loads
When her necklace of pearls was made,
And to furnish the hide of her dainty shoes
A deer had been shot in a glade.

She wore a lot of amber rings
With flies trapped in the latter;
A civit was minced to mix her scent–
But what did a civit matter?
Eva beneath the Serpent Tree
Was combing her sulphurous hair,
When the Serpent slid down Its enamelled length,
And gave her a wicked stare.

"To tempt you I've come," the Serpent said,
"To provoke you and make you bold."
And It looked with a smile, remembering
An earlier Eve of gold,

And how simple it was to turn people bad,
Reinvoking the ancient Curse.
But Eva only laughed, and had
The Serpent made into a purse.

La Dame

'The game is done! I've won! I've won!'
Quoth she, and whistles thrice.

The Ancient Mariner
Coleridge

f the land, and what the land gave you–war, pestilence, hunger, pain–he had had enough. It was the sea he wanted. The sea he went looking for. His grandfather had been a fisherman, and he had been taken on the ships in his boyhood. He remembered enough. He had never been afraid. Not of water, still or stormy. It was the ground he had done with, full of graves and mud.

His name was Jeluc, and he had been a soldier fourteen of his twenty-eight years. He looked a soldier as he walked into the village above the sea.

Some ragged children playing with sticks called out foul names after him. And one ran up and said, "Give us a coin."

"Go to hell," he answered, and the child let him alone. It was not a rich village.

The houses huddled one against another. But at the end of the struggling, straggling street, a long stone pier went out and over the beach, out into the water. On the beach there were boats lying in the slick sand, but at the end of the pier was a ship, tied fast, dipping slightly, like a swan.

She was pale as ashes, and graceful, pointed and slender, with a single mast, the yard across it with a sail the colour of turned milk bound up. She would take a crew of three, but one man could handle her. She had a little cabin with a hollow window and door.

Birds flew scavenging round and round the beach; they sat on the house roofs between, or on the boats. But none alighted on the ship.

Jeluc knocked on the first door. No one came. He tried the second and third doors, and at the fourth a woman appeared, sour and scrawny.

"What is it?" She eyed him like the Devil. He was a stranger.

"Who owns the pale ship?"

"The ship? Is Fatty's ship."

"And where would I find Fatty?"

"From the wars, are you?" she asked. He said nothing. "I have a boy to the wars. He never came back."

Jeluc thought, Poor bitch. Your son's making flowers in the muck. But then, the thought, What would he have done here?

He said again, "Where will I find Fatty?"

"Up at the drinking-house," she said, and pointed.

He thanked her and she stared. Probably she was not often thanked.

The drinking-house was out of the village and up the hill, where sometimes you found the church. There seemed to be no church here.

It was a building of wood and bits of stone, with a sloping roof, and inside there was the smell of staleness and ale.

They all looked up, the ten or so fellows in the house, from their benches.

He stood just inside the door and said, "Who owns the pale ship?"

"I do," said the one the woman had called Fatty. He was gaunt as a rope. He said, "What's it to you?"

"You don't use her much."

"Nor I do. How do you know?"

"She has no proper smell of fish, or the birds would be at her."

"There you're wrong," said Fatty. He slurped some ale. He did have a fat mouth, perhaps that was the reason for his name. "She's respected, my lady. Even the birds respect her."

"I'll buy your ship," said Jeluc. "How much?"

All the men murmured.

Fatty said, "Not for sale."

Jeluc had expected that. He said, "I've been paid off from my regiment. I've got money here, look." And he took out some pieces of silver.

The men came round like beasts to be fed, and Jeluc wondered if they would set on him, and got ready to knock them down. But they knew him for a soldier. He was dangerous beside them, poor drunken sods.

"I'll give you this," said Jeluc to Fatty.

Fatty pulled at his big lips.

"She's worth more, my lady."

"Is that her name?" said Jeluc. "That's what men call the sea. *La Dame.* She's not worth so much, but I won't worry about that."

Fatty was sullen. He did not know what to do.

Then one of the other men said to him. "You could take that to the town. You could spend two whole nights with a whore, and drink the place dry."

"Or," said another, "you could buy the makings to mend your old house."

Fatty said, "I don't know. Is my ship. Was my dad's."

"Let her go," said another man. "She's not lucky for you. Nor for him."

Jeluc said, "Not lucky, eh? Shall I lower my price?"

"Some daft tale," said Fatty. "She's all right. I've kept her trim."

"He has," the others agreed.

"I could see," said Jeluc. He put the money on a table. "There it is."

Fatty gave him a long, bended look. "Take her, then. She's the lady."

"I'll want provisions," he said. "I mean to sail over to the islands."

A grey little man bobbed forward. "You got more silver? My wife'll see to you. Come with me."

The grey man's wife left the sack of meal, and the dried pork and apples, and the cask of water, at the village end of the pier, and Jeluc carried them out to the ship.

Her beauty impressed him as he walked towards her. To another maybe she would only have been a vessel. But he saw her lines. She was shapely. And the mast was slender and strong.

He stored the food and water, and the extra things, the ale and rope and blankets, the pan for hot coals, in the cabin. It was bare, but for its cupboard and the wooden bunk. He lay here a moment, trying it. It felt familiar as his own skin.

The deck was clean and scrubbed, and above the tied sail was bundled on the creaking yard, whiter than the sky. He checked her over. Nothing amiss.

The feel of her, dipping and bobbing as the tide turned, gave him a wonderful sensation of escape.

He would cast off before sunset, get out on to the sea, in case the oafs of the village had any amusing plans. They were superstitious of the ship, would not use her but possibly did not like to see her go. She was their one elegant thing, like a madonna in the church, if they had had one.

Her name was on her side, written dark.

The wind rose as the leaden sun began to sink.

He let down her sail, and it spread like a swan's wing. It

was after all discoloured, of course, yet from a distance it would look very white. Like a woman's arm that had freckles when you saw it close.
The darkness came, and by then the land was out of sight. All the stars swarmed up, brilliant, as the clouds melted away. A glow was on the tips of the waves, such as he remembered. Tomorrow he would set lines for fish, baiting them with scraps of pork.

He cooked his supper of meal cakes on the coals, then lit a pipe of tobacco. He watched the smoke go up against the stars, and listened to the sail, turning a little to the wind.

The sea made noises, rushes and stirrings, and sometimes far away would come some sound, a soft booming or a slender cry, such as were never heard on land. He did not know what made these voices, if it were wind or water, or some creature. Perhaps he had known in his boyhood, for it seemed he recalled them.

When he went to the cabin, leaving the ship on her course, with the rope from the tiller tied to his waist, he knew that he would sleep as he had not slept on the beds of the earth.

The sea too was full of the dead, but they were a long way down. Theirs was a clean finish among the mouths of fishes.

He thought of mermaids swimming alongside, revealing their breasts, and laughing at him that he did not get up and look at them.

He slept.

Jeluc dreamed he was walking down the stone pier out of the village. It was starlight, night, and the pale ship was tied there at the pier's end as she had been. But between him and the ship stood a tall gaunt figure. It was not Fatty or the grey man, for as Jeluc came near, he saw it wore a black robe, like a priest's, and a hood concealed all its skull face but for a broad white forehead.

As he got closer, Jeluc tried to see the being's face, but

could not. Instead a white thin hand came up and plucked from him a silver coin.

It was Charon, the Ferryman of the Dead, taking his fee.

Jeluc opened his eyes.

He was in the cabin of the ship called *La Dame,* and all was still, only the music of the water and the wind, and through the window he saw the stars sprinkle by.

The rope at his waist gave its little tug, now this way, now that, as it should. All was well.

Jeluc shut his eyes.

He imagined his lids weighted by silver coins.

He heard a soft voice singing, a woman's voice. It was very high and sweet, not kind, no lullaby.

In the morning he was tired, although his sleep had gone very deep. But it had been a long walk he had had to the village.

He saw to the lines, baiting them carefully, and went over the ship, but she was as she should be. He cooked some more cakes, and ate a little of the greasy pork. The ale was flat and bitter, but he had tasted far worse.

He stood all morning by the tiller.

The weather was brisk but calm enough, and at this rate he would sight the first of the islands by the day after tomorrow. He might be sorry at that, but then he need not linger longer. He could be off again.

In the afternoon he drowsed. And when he woke, the sun was over to the west like a bullet in a dull dark rent in the sky.

Jeluc glimpsed something. He turned, and saw three thin men with ragged dripping hair, who stood on the far side of the cabin on the afterdeck. They were quite still, colourless and dumb. Then they were gone.

Perhaps it had been some formation of the clouds, some shadow cast for a moment by the sail. Or his eyes, playing tricks.

But he said aloud to the ship, "Are you haunted, my dear? Is that your secret?"

When he checked his lines, he had caught nothing, but there was no law which said he must.

The wind dropped low and, as yesterday, the clouds dissolved when the darkness fell, and he saw the stars blaze out like diamonds, but no moon.

It seemed to him he should have seen her, the moon, but maybe some little overcast had remained, or he had made a mistake.

He concocted a stew with the pork and some garlic and apple, ate, smoked his pipe, listened to the noises of the sea.

He might be anywhere. A hundred miles from any land. He had seen no birds all day.

Jeluc went to the cabin, tied the rope, and lay down. He slept at once. He was on the ship, and at his side sat one of his old comrades, a man who had died from a cannon shot two years before. He kept his hat over the wound shyly, and said to Jeluc, "Where are you bound? The islands? Do you think you'll get there?"

"This lady'll take me there," said Jeluc.

"Oh, she'll take you somewhere."

Then the old soldier showed him the compass, and the needle had gone mad, reared up and poked down, right down, as if indicating hell.

Jeluc opened his eyes and the rope twitched at his waist, this way, that.

He got up, and walked out on to the deck.

The stars were bright as white flames, and the shadow of the mast fell hard as iron on the deck. But it was all wrong.

Jeluc looked up, and on the mast of the ship hung a wiry man, with his long grey hair all tangled round the yard and trailing down the sail, crawling on it, like the limbs of a spider.

This man Jeluc did not know, but the man grinned, and he began to pull off silver rings from his fingers and cast them at Jeluc. They fell with loud cold notes. A huge round moon, white as snow, rose behind the apparition. Its hand tugged and tugged, and Jeluc heard it curse. The finger had come off with the ring, and fell on his boot.

"What do you want with me?" said Jeluc, but the man on the mast faded, and the severed finger was only a drop of spray.

Opening his eyes again, Jeluc lay on the bunk, and he smelled a soft warm perfume. It was like flowers on a summer day. It was the aroma of a woman.

"Am I awake now?"

Jeluc got up, and stood on the bobbing floor, then he went outside. There was no moon, and only the sail moved on the yard.

One of the lines was jerking, and he went to it slowly. But when he tested it, nothing was there.

The smell of heat and plants was still faintly about him, and now he took it for the foretaste of the islands, blown out to him.

He returned to the cabin and lay wakeful, until near dawn he slept and dreamed a mermaid had come over the ship's rail. She was pale as pale, with ash blonde hair, and he wondered if it would be feasible to make love to her, for she had a fish's tail, and no woman's parts at all that he could see.

Dawn was so pale it seemed the ship had grown darker. She had a sort of flush, her sides and deck, her smooth mast, her outspread sail.

He could not scent the islands anymore.

Rain fell, and he went into the cabin, and there examined his possessions, as once or twice he had done before a battle. His knife, his neckscarf of silk, which a girl had given him years before, a lucky coin he had kept without believing in it, a bullet that had missed him and gone into a tree. His money, his boots, his pipe. Not much.

Then he thought that the ship was now his possession, too, *his* lady.

He went and stood in the rain and looked at her.

There was nothing on the lines.

He ate pork for supper.

The rain eased, and in the cabin, he slept.

The woman stood at the tiller.

She rested her hand on it, quietly.

She was very pale, her hair long and blonde, and her old-fashioned dress the shade of good paper.

He stood and watched her for some time, but she did not respond, although he knew she was aware of him, and that he watched. Finally he walked up to her, and she turned her head.

She was very thin, her face all bones, and she had great glowing pale gleaming eyes, and these stared now right through him.

She took her hand off the tiller and put it on his shoulder, and he felt her touch go through him like her look, straight down his body, through his heart, belly and loins, and out at his feet.

He thought, She'll want to go into the cabin with me.

So he gave her his arm.

They walked, along the deck, and he let her pass into the cabin first.

She turned about, as she had turned her head, slowly, looking at everything, the food and the pan of coals, which did not burn now, the blankets on the bunk.

Then she moved to the bunk and lay down, on her back, calm as any woman who had done such a thing a thousand times.

Jeluc went to her at once, but he did not wait to undo his clothing. He found, surprising himself, that he lay down on top of her, straight down, letting her frail body have all his weight, his chest on her bosom, his loins on her loins, but separated by their garments, legs on her legs. And last of all, his face on her face, his lips against hers.

Rather than lust it was the sensuality of a dream he felt, for of course it was a dream. His whole body sweetly ached, and the centre of joy seemed at his lips rather than anywhere else, his lips that touched her lips, quite closed, not even moist nor very warm.

Light delicious spasms passed through him, one after another, ebbing, flowing, resonant, and ceaseless.

He did not want to change it, did not want it to end. And it did not end.

But eventually, he seemed to drift away from it, back into sleep. And this was so comfortable that, although he regretted the sensation's loss, he did not mind so much.

When he woke, he heard them laughing at him. Many men, laughing, low voices and higher ones, coarse and rough as if torn from tin throats and voice boxes of rust. "He's going the same way."

"So he is too."

Going the way that they had gone. The three he had seen on the deck, the one above the sail.

It was the ship. The ship had him.

He got up slowly, for he was giddy and chilled. Wrapping one of the blankets about him, he stepped out into the daylight.

The sky was white with hammerheads of black. The sea had a dull yet oily glitter.

He checked his lines. They were empty. No fish had come to the bait, as no birds had come to the mast.

He gazed back over the ship.

She was no longer pale. No, she was rosy now. She had a dainty blush to her, as if of pleasure. Even the sail was like the petal of a rose.

An old man stood on the afterdeck and shook his head and vanished.

Jeluc thought of lying on the bunk, facedown, and his vital juices or their essence draining into the wood. He could not avoid it. Everywhere here he must touch her. He could not lie to sleep in the sea.

He raised his head. No smell of land.

By now, surely, the islands should be in view, up against those clouds there– But there was nothing. Only the water on all sides and below, and the cold sky above, and over that, the void.

During the afternoon, as he watched by the tiller for the land, Jeluc slept.

He found that he lay with his head on her lap, and she was lovely now, prettier than any woman he had ever known. Her hair was honey, and her dress like a rose. Her white skin flushed with health and in her cheeks and lips three flames. Her eyes were dark now, very fine. They shone on him.

She leaned down, and covered his mouth with hers.

Such bliss–

He woke.

He was lying on his back, he had rolled, and the sail tilted over his face.

He got up, staggering, and trimmed the sail.

Jeluc attended to the ship.

The sunset came and a ghost slipped round the cabin, hiding its sneering mouth with its hand.

Jeluc tried to cook a meal, but he was clumsy and scorched his fingers. As he sucked them, he thought of her kisses. If kisses were what they were.

No land.

The sun set. It was a dull grim sky, with a hole of whiteness that turned grey, yet the ship flared up.

She was red now, *La Dame,* her cabin like a live coal, her sides like wine, her sail like blood.

Of course, he could keep awake through the night. He

had done so before. And tomorrow he would sight the land.

He paced the deck, and the stars came out, white as ice. Or knives. There was no moon.

He marked the compass, saw to the sail, set fresh meat on the lines that he knew no fish would touch.

Jeluc sang old songs of his campaigns, but hours after he heard himself sing, over and over:

"She the ship
"She the sea
"She the she."

His grandfather had told him stories of the ocean, of how it was a woman, a female thing, and that the ships that went out upon it were female also, for it would not stand any human male to go about on it unless something were between him and–her. But the sea was jealous too. She did not like women, true human women, to travel on ships. She must be reverenced, and now and then demanded sacrifice.

His grandfather had told him how, once, they had had to throw a man overboard, because he spat into the sea. It seemed he had spat a certain way, or at the wrong season. He had had, too, the temerity to learn to swim, which few sailors were fool enough to do. It had taken a long while for him to go down. They had told the widow the water washed him overboard.

Later, Jeluc believed that the ship had eyes painted on her prow, and these saw her way, but now they closed. She did not care where she went. And then too he thought she had a figurehead, like a great vessel of her kind, and this was a woman who clawed at the ship's sides, howling.

But he woke up, in time.

He kept awake all night.

In the morning the sun rose, lax and pallid as an ember, while the ship burned red as fire.

Jeluc looked over and saw her red reflection in the dark water.

There was no land on any side.

He made a breakfast of undercooked meal cakes, and ate a little. He felt her tingling through the soles of his boots.

He tested the sail and the lines, her tiller, and her compass. There was something odd with its needle.

No fish gave evidence of themselves in the water, and no birds flew overhead.

The sea rolled in vast glaucous swells.

He could not help himself. He slept.

There were birds!

He heard them calling, and looked up.

The sky, pale grey, a cinder, was full of them, against a sea of stars that were too faint for night.

And the birds, so black, were gulls. And yet, they were gulls of bone. Their beaks were shut like needles. They wheeled and soared, never alighting on the mast or yard or rails of the ship.

I'm dreaming, God help me. God wake me—

The gulls swooped over and on, and now, against the distant diluted dark, he saw the tower of a lighthouse rising. It was the land, at last, and he was saved.

But oh, the lighthouse sent out its ray, and from the opposing side there came another, the lamp flashing out. And then another, and another. They were before him and behind him, and all round. The lit points of them crossed each other on the blank sombre sparkle of the sea. A hundred lighthouses, sending their signals to hell.

Jeluc stared around him. And then he heard the deep roaring in the ocean bed, a million miles below.

And one by one, the houses of the light sank, they went into the water, their long necks like Leviathan's, and vanished in a cream of foam.

All light was gone. The birds were gone.

She came, then.

She was beautiful now. He had never, maybe, seen a beautiful woman.

Her skin was white, but her lips were red. And her hair was the red of gold. Her gown was the red of winter berries. She walked with a little gliding step.

"Lady," he said, "you don't want me."

But she smiled.

Then he looked beyond the ship, for it felt not right to him, and the sea was all lying down. It was like the tide going from the shore, or, perhaps, water from a basin. It ran away, and the ship dropped after it.

And then they were still in a pale nothingness, a sort of beach of sand that stretched in all directions. Utterly becalmed.

"But I don't want the land."

He remembered what the land had given him. Old hurts, drear pains. Comrades dead. Wars lost. Youth gone.

"Not the land," he said.

But she smiled.

And over the waste of it, that sea of salt, came a shrill high whistling, once and twice and three times. Some sound of the ocean he had never heard.

Then she had reached him. Jeluc felt her smooth hands on his neck. He said, "Woman, let me go into the water, at least." But it was no use. Her lips were soft as roses on his throat.

He saw the sun rise, and it was red as red could be. But then, like the ship in his dream, he closed his eyes. He thought, But there was no land.

There never is.

The ship stood fiery crimson on the rising sun, that lit her like a bonfire. Her sides, her deck, her cabin, her mast and sail, like fresh pure blood.

Presently the sea, which moved under her in dark silk, began to lip this blood away.

At first, it was only a reflection in the water, but next it was a stain, like heavy dye.

The sea drank from the colour of the ship, for the sea too was feminine and a devourer of men.

The sea drained *La Dame* of every drop, so gradually she turned back paler and paler into a vessel like ashes.

And when the sea had sucked everything out of her, it let her go, the ship, white as a bone, to drift away down the morning.

The Pretty Knife

Part One

There is a saying in the Red Hills:

When do you need a Pretty Knife? You need the Pretty Knife when you go to kill one of the most beautiful things on earth.

Or one of the most ugly.

1

The Tyrant had ruled the land for more than fifty years, though he looked young still, not more than thirty. But then, he was a very able sorcerer. Served by Minions and Terrors beyond the imagination of any who wished not to go mad, he had had an easy time of it.

In the beginning he had stood first on the highest of the mountains, which was called Mount Onyx. And from there, with his pale green eyes, he had viewed and assessed the terrain. Then at his command fiends and demons, impossible monsters of which no true description can be made since they were and are irreconcilable to the minds of men, swept from the sky–that turned to blood and bile at their arrival. They decimated the land at his order. And after that few could or would go against him.

Following this awful time, which was subsequently known as the Great Deliverance, the majority of the survivors, having no choice, maintained their country for *him* and *only* for him.

His name was Korond.

When a legend lives on, especially in the form of a powerful and charismatic male, whose eyes are like green stars, hair like a saffron river, with a tender smile like love, and a chastising look like *death*–what can any people do but give in? True, now and then at first, rebellion kindled.

But any plan for liberation he thwarted, or his army of undermages did so, (particularly the mage known as Qo.)While at one whisper of Korond's musical voice hell poured from the air, or out of the ground, or from anywhere, as the fancy took him.

Who can fight such fires, such lightnings?

Only fools, brave as gods. Only god-like fools.

The land was plaqued and armoured with their burned and broken bones, and then came peace, the pacifism of surrender and negation.

But in concealment they prayed. *Deliver us.*

If Korond heard he paid no attention.

To him such murmurings were like soft rain that is not even wet.

2

Huth was returning to the village of Onyx, over the hills below the mountain. Dawn had already begun, changing the flower-softened slopes to copper and crimson. But behind them, the crag never altered. It stayed black as a polished coal. The story had it Korond had alighted there at the start, and there mapped out the land for his conquest. No wonder the mountain now was always black–the colour of empty starless night, and human despair.

The hunting had been fine. It generally was, and there was a good reason for that. Huth was still lightly brushing shed loose gilded hairs from himself, when a nearby sound alerted him.

He became the epitome of silence and stillness.

And out of a brake of summer trees stepped Xcuu, the heaven-watcher. .

"Is it you, Huth?" asked Xcuu, smiling mildly. In the sun's just-minted rays his face was fully knowing, yet he never said what he knew. He glanced merely at the dead hill-antelope over Huth's broad shoulders. The kill was clean, and all the village of Onyx would benefit from the meat.

Xcuu continued: "I have seen a pattern tonight in the constellations, like sixteen diamonds circling in four rings."

Huth nodded. "This world is made of patterns, sir. The sea when it runs in to shore forms patterns in the waves. Clouds do, that powder the sky. Birth and love and death–all these are like woven threads. If we could only see it, sir, I think the secret of life itself would be a pattern, perhaps... like a twisting spiral of jewels."

Xcuu had observed Huth closely as he gave his reply. Xcuu nodded. "Such patterns I have noted. Now this pattern, the meaning of which is direct. A child has been born during the night. In sixteen years she will be a woman."

Huth waited, considering. The pronouncement, even for the heaven-watching sage Xcuu, was very strange.

"In sixteen years," Huth said quietly, "I shall be thirty-two years old. *Too* old, surely, to marry the girl."

"Ah," said Xcuu, "she is not for marrying. She is God's answer to our prayers. Huth, listen, she is the *Pretty Knife.* "

3

Nothing overtly untoward had graced or made ominous the birth of Isilmi.

She came of a fawn-haired clan, and her light brown hair hung long from earliest childhood. Her skin was pale and her eyes smoke-blue. As the years passed she grew up slim and strong, and while not beautiful, she had a pleasing, notable face, female rather than feminine.

To the village of Amber, where Isilmi had been born, a straight-backed, black-eyed old man had journeyed in her fourth year. He was named Xcuu, a sage from over the mountain, and he presently took her parents aside. To begin with they thought he might be unhinged, but from various supernatural powers he demonstrated, (the calling up of a dead ancestor to concur in his own assessment–the mending of a fractured arm by touch) both the parents, and all the fawn clan, came to accept his judgements, even that concerning the girl-child.

It seemed she must be taught not only to read and write, to study and to learn, and this by Xcuu himself, but also from the village warriors all the arts of combat.

Although not one of the men had lifted a blade in anger for more than fifty years, they had kept their talent in case of need. For despite the intolerable, impassive Tyrancy of Korond, other enemies might appear, and no doubt Korond would send no help. He existed only to envampirise the land, and dwelled himself at the land's deepest centre, a mysterious valley some miles below sea level. He had long since had built there a fantastic city, called Vay Ezb, the myths of which few could confirm, but which were equally marvellous and horrible. To this dire place it seemed Isilmi was eventually herself to travel. She was to be the land's rescuer, the people's *Jaafpegwe*–an ancient title which might indicate either a saviour or the magic of a saving spell.

By the time she was fifteen the young woman was an

acccomplished scholar and fighter, both. She knew every tale, history and custom, and could enact every move of duel or battle-play with consummate skill. No man, let alone woman, could best her. Beside all this, she had been well-prepared by Xcuu to learn her role in life, how to accept it with a still passion, excluding all others. And as well, to recognise her own glory, her greatness, implicitly, yet lacking every vanity or silliness. Almost, then, she was ready.

4

It was late on a night of full moon that Xcuu returned across the ledges of the mountain, and walked down toward the villages of Onyx and Emerald. Between the two, on another hill, he found–as he had known he would–the blacksmith's forge and dwelling, a cave-like building set in the hillside, but with an epic view at its entry of any sun or moon-rise. Here Xcuu sat to wait for dawn, and Huth, who was now the blacksmith and metal-worker in his father's stead. Almost sixteen years had passed. In terrible Vay Ezb, they told you, Korond, (now sixty-six years in situ) remained with the beautiful male looks of thirty. But then the hills had not changed much, silvered and steel-blued by a yet high moon. Nor was old Xcuu much changed either, in appearance or character. He sat on the turf and watched the heaven, and recalled an old song of his youth. Which youth had been an unconscionable age before. Then he dozed, until a marigold colour began to rework the iron sky. Day was coming back, and, too, Huth was coming back, striding down the slope with a pair of deer now slung over his back. Huth had grown to be a stocky, splendid man, hair like the new bronze he sometimes forged for ritual daggers. (For true war, though there had been none since the last rebellion was crushed, daggers were made from night-black iron, or moon-blued steel.)

Huth checked when he saw the old man. Once seen *never*

forgotten.

"Greetings, sir. What can I do for you?"

Xcuu smiled. He had glimpsed an immense golden whisker lying caught on Huth's tough arm. Xcuu was too tactful to mention this.

"The time is almost upon us. Do you remember?"

"Sixteen years," said Huth, letting go the deer in the grass. "I remember. All the villages have murmurs of it. Is she real then, the special girl, scholar and warrior, pure as a priestess, vital as a constellation in four rings?"

"Yes," said Xcuu. "But she lacks one thing for her task."

Huth gazed at him.

In his guts Huth knew, had known somehow for months, as if a night-flying moth had scribbled the words against his ear in sleep.

"She must have," said Xcuu, "her blade. The most fabulous and perfect ever forged. How else can she act out her role? Not with any ordinary knife. For this work she, the only one able to slay Korond, as the stars advised, must not only *be*, but must *wield* the Pretty Knife."

5

Huth forged the knife. It took him three months. This because of his researches into and after the metal, his care with it, the correct fires and waters, even the dousings of blood, milk and wine.

The Knife was not only *pretty*, it was of a resplendent loveliness. The sun, the moon and the stars seemed to live in its blade, that was like a static wave of the sea, held in purest glass and lit by every possible sky–at all seasons, times of day and night.

The haft was of silver hardened almost like the steel blade, and ribbed with each metal known to mankind.

No one ever could have seen such a knife before.

Not many did now.

After Huth, and Xcuu, only *she* was to see it, Isilmi, Jaafpegwe, saviour, star-predicted.

Only she–and, of course, one other. Korond would see the Pretty Knife, as Isilmi, the only one able in all worlds to kill him, put out forever his immortal life.

6

Isilmi herself, from the instant of being told, (at eight years of age) recognised and grasped her function.

It was her reason for being designated by God to be born. The constellations, the sky-signs by which God could show his requests, his orders, and his answers, had defined precisely that Isilmi, of all humanity, was capable of destroying Korond.

Why the signs did not display.

But to a believer and sage such as Xcuu, that small item did not matter.

Exactly as Korond, the evil sorcerer, had erupted from nowhere to take possession of them all, so had Isilmi entered the world, the counterbalance, to put all right.

This truth Xcuu had instilled in her heart and mind. Her soul, it went without saying, must already understand, and simply needed a reminder.

Isilmi was not afraid, but neither was she vainglorious. With calm, steady intent she had striven towards her goal.

That night, when Xcuu brought to her the Pretty Knife, she accepted it on her open palms, and then bent to kiss the exquisite blade. She recognised the Knife, also. It was her focus, her genius made manifest.

When she left the village of Amber she had no regrets. Already she lived in the rarity of otherness. The wonderful world, to which she was far from impervious, filled her with a sweet yearning to protect. Perhaps what a mother might feel for a child–or, more logically, a *child* for its beloved *mother.*

As she walked inward through the geography of the land, seeking those lower rifts that finally condensed in the bizarre city of Vay Ezb, Isilmi experienced no qualms. She trusted utterly what she was. She *loved* what she was. Without hubris, without self-blindness.

In all unclouded honesty, she did not even bother if she herself should be slain during the slaughter of Korond. It would not hinder her. For before and beyond physical existence, huge continents of *otherlife* extended. But her role and her goal were paramount.

She was naturally endowed with endurance and strength, and glowing youthful ardour–no less sparkling for being contained in self-awareness and entirely selfless power. And therefore she strode up and down the undulations of the land, through forests thick-summered with jade-green foliage, across narrow bridges and stone-laid roads or tracks of trampled dirt. She beheld huge cats and wide-pinioned birds, tiny fish like ruby sequins and snakes like moving ropes of peridot and sulphur. Through groves of lamplike fruit she went, and into rock tunnels blacker than the Mountain of Onyx. She crossed a lake like an indigo mirror.

She slept in trees, or under village roofs on mattresses of straw. The people here, so distant from Amber, Emerald and Onyx, did not know her. She was glad for them that they did not–to keep them safe. Glad too for herself, for she deeply loved what she was, and perhaps jealously, a little, liked to have become *unknown.*

The summer waned to a fall of metallic leaves, as she walked.

Clear air, palest blue crystal skies, the winds turning with an edge of frost. A knife's edge, and pretty–

No more villages appeared.

In another four days she would see it, miles below, down the pink-grey steps of the stilly tumbling rift: his city. Vay Ezb. The ultimate scene of his drama, hers.

7

Vay Ezb was reached by a flight of stairs. They were of polished marble, but they *moved.* No sooner had a foot been set on them than the whole assemblage began slowly to slide downwards. The traveller need only stand there then and patiently wait and he would reach, in about the half of one hour, the subsea valley of the city. Unless of course he leapt off in alarm. Many had fallen to their deaths through doing that, since the stair commenced at the brink of a cliff.

Perhaps inevitably only a scatter of persons sought and entered the city now. All of these had their reasons, which were frequently profane. But Vay Ezb welcomed such celebrities: the man who murdered strangers out of artistic malice, the woman who had eaten her children alive–such types.

And there were others who visited the metropolis. Men and women also partially fiends, for Korond's mages had now and then bred an assortment of these beings on human captives. And otherwise Korond's presence in the area could often attract wandering entities, demonish and foul, that if he had been absent would never have ventured in. There were his servants as well, those grisly acolytes spontaneously available to him and quite beyond description. Thus, the population of Vay Ezb.

But it was beautiful, the city. (Just as Korond was.)

It too might be one of the most beautiful things on earth. Though one of the most ugly.

Isilmi reached the cliff near midnight, and stepped on to the stair.

She had put on the dark robe of an itinerant priest. The Pretty Knife lay in a closed scabbard of onyx that she wore under the robe, and hanging like a heavy pendant at her throat. Occasionally priests did come to the city, the sort that venerated sinister spirits. They would have crimes and macabre obsessions to celebrate. Village belief was full of this.

Yet really, so much was rumoured of Vay Ezb, and so little *properly* known.

Isilmi was calm as quiet water.

She rode the stair, and gazed below, and up and down and all about, as she descended.

8

Qo, the foremost magus of the Tyrant Korond, was no watcher of heaven. *Qo* was a watcher of the world.

Far up in a red-gold edifice that passed as the palace of his master, Qo would go to squat before a sort of reflective web. In this, in little pockets and discs, Qo could, through his impressive occult gifts, perceive fragments of the earth. But mostly, in a huge mirroring gem at the web's centre, he was enabled, (after intense concentration), to view the entire life of the hell-city.

To him its daily, nightly existence was presented as scintillant lines and writhings of colour and violent consciousness. It was like a stupendous woven cloth, but all *alive*. And always within it the most appalling acts appeared as delightful clusters of jewellery, or breathtaking pyrotechnics. Even thoughts, when sufficiently incongruous, crazed, depraved, or ennightmared, showed in the way spring flowers do, appearing joyfully from blank soil.

Tonight, nevertheless, Qo spied some apparition in his mage-glass that was unlike anything he had ever noted in the city.

For a while he gaped at it, shifting his ungainly body from one haunch to the other, made physically uncomfortable at this peculiar and unwholesome aberration.

It flowed like a slender river. It negotiated all the fiery rocks and pedestals of vivid vile liveliness. A moving thread of silky *difference* drawing always nearer.

9

But *she* saw towers tall as the moon, maybe, up the glittering sides of which objects and elements crawled, flew, and otherwise wended. And pits she saw, dropping down and down, and full of a million lights, as if decorated by outsized fire-flies. A tide, like that of a sea, but made of cumulous, moved through the thoroughfares, violet and owl-eye yellow, or sometimes scarlet. As the levels drew in about her, Isilmi beheld creatures with snake-hair and blood-red eyes, and man-like spiderisms that scuttled on twelve or thirteen legs, and formless, shimmering beasts from which she turned her eyes, as even the spiders and snake-hairs did. Chambers piled one on another, resembling rather the honey-cells in a beehive. Spouting waters ran upwards, and trees grew down, and vines with grasping claws scratched unreadable graffiti on platinum walls. Forms that might, sometimes, be human, but mostly might *never* be anything of the sort, dined, or performed sexual acts, or sang. Once a flock of squeaking bluish leaves settled on Isilmi, but she brushed them away with so little panic they shrivelled and flaked off in ash. No doubt anger or fright would have swollen them up like leaches.

The stair was grounded at last, ringed all around by the spangled heights and abysses.

Isilmi was not afraid. She stayed cool. This was a facet of her predestined role. She walked into the city's mass, until she arrived at the margin of a colossal plaza. Activities went on here also, most incomprehensible, many of a bewildering, glamorous dreadfulness.

Across a surface like a pane of crinkled glass, under which amorphalities roiled, rose a vast golden house: the palace of Korond. No one could mistake it.

It had eyes, too, the palace, great, ice-green eyes all along its upper terraces, which stared outwards, and intermittently blinked or winked... or momentarily closed, as if to savour some extreme sight just witnessed.

10

Entering one of the massive chambers of his master, Qo took no notice at all of its impressive scope and ornamentation. This was in some ways to evidence the mage's respect for Korond. But also, if the truth were to be said, it reflected Qo's uninterest in the evidence of something so *completely* evil, to which he, Qo, was so utterly used.

"Unimaginable Lord," said Qo, bowing down.

Korond did not even turn his head.

He reclined on a couch that had the shape of two carved ivory lions. He was *not* lion-like, more serpentine, perhaps, in this evening's garment of jet-black scales. His corn-yellow hair fountained over the cushions. His pale green eyes were nearly shut. He was beautiful as ecstasy. His looks could make the unwary drunk.

But Qo was not unwary.

Qo knew a thing or two.

"Well?" asked Korond after a while.

"In my tracking mirror, sire, I have found a curiosity."

"Yes?"

"Are you to go out tonight, into the plaza?" inquired Qo.

"If I am?"

Qo said, "Something has gained access to Vay Ezb that is not like anything I have ever seen here, and seldom anywhere. There is no *wickedness* to it. It is not *poisoned*, nor corrupted, nor crippled by the cruelties of the world. It does not hate, or mourn. It does not greedily *want.* Across the glistering scheme of your city, it has run like a slender stream of pure, clear water. It stands out on the canvas of Vay Ezb like a pearl dropped on purple velvet–just as, my Unimaginable Lord, you incandesce here like black fire burning on red."

Korond lazily smiled. He enjoyed flattery. It provoked him.

"What does this weirdness want then, Qo? And what *is* it?"

"I have no notion what it is, though I think it will be instantly apparent to me when I approach it–strong as the scent of cinnamon. What it *wants*, I have no doubt, is you, great lord."

"My humble self?" Sinuous, Korond the lizard stretched. "Why? For what?"

Qo glided near and whispered. His words were in some other, inconceivable tongue.

Korond listened. His eyes opened wide and he grinned. Even his grin was entirely beautiful.

11

Hollowed rams' horns were blown, two hours before sunrise. The plaza before the palace reverberated. (The mechanical green eyes that watched from above let go tears of molten verdigris, that struck the square like paint or, having hardened on the way down, broke in bits.)

The Unimaginable Lord was about to appear to his city.

From all points of the compass of Vay Ezb creatures and emanations hurtled, longing only to look at him, to *serve* his presence.

The plaza grew yet more luminous, packed and tensed, buzzing and purring with unspeakable lusts and worshippings.

One tiny cool island remained. It was located beneath a frightful tree, that had a carapace like a stone-white crab, and rattling spikes for leaves. But the coolness had not been discomposed by the frightful tree, nor had the tree, which was quite capable of it, attacked what stood beneath. It was Isilmi standing there, grave and collected. She was–*even now*–

fearless. She had known he must come out, if not tonight or tomorrow, then soon enough. He *must* come out because he and she were the two opposing events, like twin images fashioned from one material, then separated and cast, one in a volcano, one in the upper sky.

And Isilmi knew she was the Pretty Knife, and she carried the Pretty Knife around her neck. She had only to wait, as already she had through sixteen years, and then on the long walk to Vay Ezb, and tonight on the descending stair.

And now the Tyrant arrived.

The palace doors had flared open, two wings of sunburst two hours before the dawn.

Isilmi raised her head. She scanned what strode out on the glassy paving. She did not guess that her own potent uniqueness had also been detectible, evaluated, and labelled. Or that she stood out on the boardgame of the city like a pearl on purple, like soundlessness piercing through a torrent of noise.

As Korond began to move forward, gracious as ever, he performed certain accustomed acts. He slew a few beings that rushed to reverence him, and they perished shrieking with agony, not to mention the pleasure of having been singled out. He also cast various toys to the adoring crowds. These playthings, all rainbowed and iridescent, were helpful too–a delicate, unbreakable flask–or painful–a spinning globe that stung.

The surges and bellowing of the throng, despite everything, did somewhat interrupt Isilmi's concentration. One moment the Tyrant was almost a quarter mile from her, and then, suddenly, he was planted not seven feet away.

His gorgeous radiance did not dismay her. She saw how alike were his eyes to those that studded the palace heights.

Bowing low as all the rest did, she had drawn the Knife from its enclosure. It was professionally gripped in her right hand, beneath the priestly sleeve. So well-trained in the choreography of battle was she, even blindfolded she could thrust home into his flesh.

Isilmi alone could slay Korond.

The stars–*God*–had written this message on the night of her birth.

She stood straight and gazed into his lambent face.

Not a flicker of his enchantment touched her. She was immune to everything about him, save the signal of his beating heart that only she could, forever, silence

12

The wizened and stunted man-thing, (Qo), that had appeared beside his master, whispered–in the other tongue–"*She.*"

In that moment, with a flawless fighter's spring, she was close to Korond as a lover, her hand free of her robe and folded on the glittering blade. Korond did not move. The knife, at great speed, continued to.

I am your death, she might have said.

No, he might have answered, *you are your own.*

The flying blade, formed to its one task of singular murder, should by now be hilt-deep within his breast. It was not. It had been stopped a single inch from his body.

The impact of this stop, a sorcerous barrier like solid granite, that Korond had prepared and put about him, jarred Isilmi's arm from wrist to shoulder-joint. It had hurt her unspeakably. She had dropped the knife, but she made no sound. She was stunned not only by the blow. Her destiny was fixed–yet now–undone?

Next instant a brazen lightning crashed on the plaza. Korond stood impassive within its blaze. Qo also, naturally.

Here and there all around, those creatures which caught the lightning's edges, flared and shrivelled and went out. But Isilmi changed to a statue of opal flame, and when the flame died she was a pillar of salt which–at a word from Korond–

slipped inward and down and became a simple shapeless gobbet of bitumen, lying there unalive and ended. On the perfect unsullied glass floor of the plaza in Vay Ezb.

13

By night, an air-legion of monstrous winged demonites thrummed into the skies above the villages of Amber, Emerald, Iron and Ultramarine.

Through some filthy kinetic knack Qo had learned, approximately, the region from which the would-be assassin had come.

Therefore Korond sent his sky-force to the spot.

A while they rained down fire and brimstone.

Detonations rang, walls crumbled and melted, bones exploded into blackened dust. Storm clouds, blacker than darkness, put out the stars and turned the shrinking moon to a burnt ghost.

On the earth below nothing and no one survived.

At length, work completed to the satisfaction of the demonic overflight, they took their leave, throwing down as they did so a little black boulder.

Just clear of the ruin, it balanced on the hillside, and stuck in it, a clutch of muddled steel, silver, gold, and all the metals known to mankind. A solitary phrase had been seared along the slope. The letters were big enough to read from some distance:

Your daughter, Isilmi, and her knife.

Part Two

14

Because he knew Xcuu would search him out, (even if their meeting could serve no purpose), Huth waited for him for every night of the following month. Saving, of course, the three nights of the full moon. It was on the first night of the moon's wane that the mage-sage appeared. Huth stood watching him climb the steep hill. On this flank of the mountain there was no longer any real evidence of the massacre that had occurred on its far side.

Earlier however, there had been a magenta sky and the turf was smirched with cinders, and calcined pieces of unthinkable things had fallen there. But later the men and women of Onyx, Huth among them, had tidied and repaired. The hills were sturdy and lasting, the sky swept itself clean. They knew, the Onyxians, how lucky they had been that neither the Tyrant, or any of his minions, had thought Onyx to be involved in Isilmi's treason.

Huth understood he himself was particularly fortunate. He had made the Knife, yet nothing sought to destroy him. His relief was rivalled only by an almost intolerable guilt.

Now, meeting Xcuu, Huth felt an urge to strike him.

But Xcuu was himself protected by his own magics. How else had *he* escaped the spies and wrath of Korond?

Xcuu, old as the rocks, but not even breathing quickly, reached Huth's elevated cave-veranda.

"What now?" asked Huth coldly. "Have the constellations told you some disgusting *new* sacrifice to make?"

Xcuu looked at him, then took something from the bag over his back.

"What on God's earth is that?"

"Isilmi," said Xcuu, "and the Pretty Knife."

Huth glared in total horror at the tarry, featureless bulb, and the mess of metal sticking out of it.

"Why bring this travesty to me? Have you not shamed

and mired me enough, old star-gazer? Do you want me to bury this–*wreckage*?"

"Not quite," said Xcuu. Then, perhaps only a ploy, he let Huth see how tired the old, old body was, even if the wise mind still gleamed inside it. Xcuu sat on a bench, and placed Isilmi's remains on the ground between them. "I have studied these matters," said Xcuu. "I have ascertained what none of us foresaw. How they might suss her out in their infernal city–through her utter difference to anything and anyone in Vay Ezb. Her very purity, her *veracity*, made her glow for them, for Qo especially, like a lamp in the night."

"Yes," Huth grudgingly agreed. "Her strength was her undoing. Poor child," he added. "Yet only she could kill him–because of that purity, that *singularity*. And so her fate became her death, not his."

"The fault of ignorance is mine," Xcuu replied. "But the solution had seemed so clear. Now, evidently, it *is* clear. She has had to die to make it possible."

Then Huth raged. He roared, so his voice rebounded like flung sheets of stone from the Onyx Mountain.

Xcuu sat patiently, and waited.

When eventually Huth ran out of rage and blasphemies sufficient to his sentiments, Xcuu paused only a few seconds, before explaining to him the rest of the riddle.

15

This time, he worked cursing.

It did not spoil either the smithing or the artistry, while the magery, (being now intrinsic), paid his human anguish no heed.

In the fire-flicked shadows of the forge, all the while Xcuu sat watching. He was, then, a watcher-of-Huth, not heaven.

Some despotic power of his moved Huth about, too, added strength to his strong arms, dexterity to his dextrous hands. He felt this, could not avoid it, as if to some extent he had been possessed by a mighty entity, a group of souls all blacksmiths, and each one also a magician.

In the end Huth gave over swearing, as he had the previous outcry before Xcuu had told him the ultimate answer.

Isilmi had been created to slay Korond. It was her motive for birth. And even now–she might accomplish the task.

"Here are her body and bones, her very hair and teeth, her destiny–*all* of her fused and condensed into this bauble of sticky dark." So Xcuu, callous and compassionate, had softly told him. "By my craft, and yours, *she* shall be reforged to a bladed weapon. And the former Knife shall supply the hilt."

"I'm no sorcerer," Huth had snarled. When he did that, Xcuu seemed to see in him what Huth also could become, when not only a mortal. "And you, old man, are no smith."

"Then we shall be two parts of a single engine. It will be done, and done very well. And then–"

"Then *what*? Some other hapless fool to go into the city of hell and–like *her*–be found out and slaughtered, and their home village put to the fire."

Xcuu shrugged, but on the air between them a flurry of malted golden fur came from nowhere, and dazzled down into the grass.

"There is *one* who can enter Vay Ezb and pass unchallenged. One who will glint in their glamorous web as if belonging to it."

Huth had altered to a block of stone.

His very heart seemed to freeze inside him.

"Oh, I've seen before you know, where others never do."

"I am a watcher, Huth. *My* role in the world."

"Be damned," said Huth. The sweat rinsed down his back.

But "You must go," Xcuu had announced, "and on one of those three significant nights. But it shall be a night of late moonrise. I will supply the chart and show you how to read it. Otherness will be all over you, and danger, like a robe of sparks. Yet you will be a man still, and able to wield the Pretty Knife that Isilmi herself must become."

"I have always had it," Huth mumbled, "since I was a boy of ten. I reckoned I was ill-wished. Then–I grew used to it."

"Be glad," said Xcuu. "You have used your gift to help the villages. Now–*now*, because of it, you can save the whole land, even perhaps, the world."

16

When the Knife was finished, that evening, Huth dreamed of Isilmi. She stood in the air, clad in gilded stuff, whole and charming. Her face was serene. She thanked him for his care in recreating her, and told him she thought the second knife even more beautiful than the first. She said she was glad the *former* Knife had not been wasted either, but had become the hilt to the blade which once, mostly, was her physical body.

"I never meant to profane you, lady," he said.

"You have not and never will."

"Shall I succeed, Isilmi? Will I kill Korond?"

But she put her finger to her lips as if this must remain unsaid, even by a phantom in a dream. Then she disappeared.

Huth, after he woke, pondered if Xcuu had sent the dream to persuade him. But Huth was already persuaded.

He got up, and drew the second Pretty Knife from its scabbard of black vitreous.

The hilt and guard, fashioned from the other weapon, were a miracle of steel and copper, tin and bronze, brass, platinum and red, white and viridian gold. But the blade was of the strangest sort.

Of *what* had *it* been forged? A straight leaf of shimmered, faceted material–it seemed created not from metal, but a blazing star. Its point coruscated light, and flashed and spat seventy colours, and then seventy more.

It was diamond. For to this the magical processes had reduced and elevated the carbonated tar of Isilmi's vanquished frame. A diamond, a star, a white sun so bright it blinded, this Pretty Knife.

The next day Huth prepared for his journey. It would take some months, and by now winter was growing close as glacial tree-bark about the earth. Which did not count for anything. Having put together what he required for travel, Huth shut up his forge and house.

Outside, he gazed for a while, as the chill morning lifted above the slopes and the mountain, staining its onyx hide for a moment the pale smouldered blue of a young woman's eyes.

And then he turned and went away.

17

He too was naturally endowed with stamina, but not of course with the glowing youthful ardour of Isilmi. *He* felt no deep feelings for the protection of the world, either paternal or filial, and his qualms were several and stern. He did not *trust* in what he was. How should he? *He* was not, as she had been meant to be, Destiny's agent. He was only one more urgent, arrogant and angry hero, cast adrift on a quest. Certainly he could die. And certainly he might also fail. His role and his goal were imposed, not inborn in him.

Geography passed him in bitter surges, and soon snow began, and the earth became a blank white page, waiting only for ink or blood or fire to write on it.

When Huth found a village lay before him, either he skirted it, or went straight through the street. He said he was a wandering blacksmith, and if they had no such man he paid them for any hospitality by smithing a day or so. Once or twice, a village and a full moon coinciding, he would carry food into the street, and share with them. He was a wandering *hunter* at those times. They marvelled at his ability. Whatever had he used to kill so swift and clean? He said it was the secret of his trade.

Later, closer to Korond's dire city, people would warn him of that fact in low fearful stammerings. As if they suspected they were always, anyway, spied on in some remote yet effective manner by the Tyrant's magicians. Huth said he had no intention of going to the city.

In the end the clusters of humanity died away, like plants lacking rain or sun. The odd deserted ruin remained, in spots, frequently stained as if by flames.

One black night made blue with stars, he took out the Knife and briefly looked at it. He asked himself if her presence might be still detectable, replied to himself that no, it would not. It was her *soul* they had scented. This was instead the essence merely of her flesh and task. After which he stared up at innumerable diamond constellations. It came to him that the four rings Xcuu had noted in the sky were not the four times four years of Isilmi's brief, terminated life as Jaafpegwe, but rather the four phases of their plot. First her birth. Next her advent at the city, her discovery and death. Then thirdly her enforced, perhaps predetermined metamorphosis into the Knife. Fourth would be Huth's use of it, and the outcome; fine, or failed.

Obdurate winter clutched the land.

But Huth realised Vay Ezb, when he saw it, would not be whitened, being shielded from snow or other weather.

In this he was correct.

18

At the core of the snow-world, Vay Ezb burned by night like a rising sun.

It turned the skies crimson during the day, a laval purple after dark.

The full moon would appear late, at the axis of midnight.

Huth had halted near to the cliff's edge. He had done this like any lost traveller, startled and marvelling at the apparition below. Afraid to advance and investigate, yet captivated by the exotic foreignness of the view.

If anything watched, (conceivably it always did), such reactions were not suspicious.

Sometime after noon, the sun masked in snow-cloud and another ice-storm beginning, Huth walked to the edge and stepped on the Stair. He was not in the least disguised. It was only that, as one or two had noticed before, at certain junctures Huth seemed even stronger than usual. His strong hair was full of metallic electricities. He had grown a short beard, which on other days was absent. Was he taller? Stockier? Maybe. When moving about he had a fluid, loping stride. Even standing still on the downward-sliding marble waterfall of stair, there was a limber and feral quality to Huth.

Descending through the layers of Vay Ezb, his eyes were a hunter's eyes, nearly thoughtless, full of a purpose known better to beasts than to most men. In shadow–the cloud-mass, some tower that shed a deeper shade–the eyes flattened and changed to amber.

By the moment he reached the floor of the rift, and sprang off on to the pavements of the city, there was a sheen and shift to Huth. It fitted into the sorcerous jigsaw of the metropolis like a jewel into its box. As Xcuu had foretold, Huth was hardly an alien, here.

Just as she had done, he traversed the thoroughfares, and entered the vast glassy plaza, above which the golden palace lifted, glaring about with eyes like cold green porcelain.

He hunkered down. Spread beneath, beside, his feet and hands were like the mighty paws of some animal. His nails had grown long, and he had sloughed both gloves and boots. He stared forwards, now and then slowly blinked. His eyes–less thoughtless, more filled by one panoramic and hungry meditation. So the big cat looks out from his cover, as he attends the presence of the deer. All over Huth, the gilt hair had risen up, grass, *fur*.

He witnessed uncountable curious and repulsive events in the plaza, but they did not, it seemed, provoke him. Conversely, though not that often, some being going by might approach, and attempt to enlist Huth's interest. But even should he glance at them, the glance was forbidding and reclusive. He excited by his persona, but did not invite. The citizens of hell drew off.

In Vay Ezb, that night, sunset was the colour of orange topaz. The cumulous-tide washed in and filled the city to the brim with its mauve and jaundice vapours.

Huth waited. By now his fingernails had altered to claws but his hands yet retained human flexibility. Would Korond come out tonight into the city? Huth, brain now set like adamant, knew that he would. Four rings had predicted it. The death of Isilmi had predicted it. And Huth's *nature*, what he *was*, this too. The balance. The counterpoise.

Across the plaza rams' horns sounded. The Unimaginable Lord was to visit them.

Huth drew himself, in one wave-like movement, to his feet.

By now his eyes were each all one amber disc, the onyx pupil small as a speck. His teeth had, every one, a lethal point. The beast Huth also was stood ready, but there remained, at least until moonrise, a man present within the beast. And he recalled quite well what hung about his neck.

19

Korond, the most beautiful, the most ugly, strolled across the crystal plaza, and his mage, Qo, hopped behind him. The all-powerful are sometimes bored. Korond was, although he did not really know it. Debatably even, the nastily semi-powerful Qo was bored. Surely some wonder might turn up out here, something worth distorting or slaughtering or engaging.

A creature came padding through the crowd towards them. "Why, look, Qo," said Korond, pleased.

Korond's garment tonight was like the ruby armour of a dragon. How radiant he was. And how radiant too the creature–all gold, it seemed, but the eyes now incarnadine, like Korond's armour.

"And who," said Korond, to the creature, "are you?"

"I am your death," said the creature, but by now it did not speak in any human tongue, however obscure. What rolled out of it was a reverberant roar, a growl. Korond did not fathom therefore its words, and Qo, who vaguely sensed them, could not translate.

So Korond, only enticed by the creature's familiarly uncanny newness, put out his elegant hand, and caressed its burning mane. And the golden creature opened a black pendant at its throat, and took out of it a thing that blazed delightfully, wildly bright as an entire constellation, crushed and compressed.

"Oh, let me see!" exclaimed Korond.

But the creature, (Huth), did not oblige. Instead he thrust forward the diamond blade with all his presently supernatural strength. And into the ruby armour it shot and pierced the breast-plate of Korond's flesh and bone, and straight into the boastful drum of Korond's heartless, inhuman heart, pinning it through and through. Out by Korond's armoured back the dagger drove, blazing now with blood. Isilmi's dagger, *Isilmi*, the Pretty Knife.

An incredible stasis congealed the plaza, invaded Vay Ezb entirely. It was as if the whole world had turned to stone.

Then, as abruptly, all and everything began to give way, to totter and crumble, to dissolve, to fall. In the midst of it Korond, however, stayed upright. He stared at Huth in amazement, even as all the lights perished. Even the very last light of all.

High roofs detached and whirled skyward–or dashed down on the streets. Walls screamed and plunged apart. Demonites and monstrosities exploded on the wing. Bits of them also splashed into the plaza. Since they had emanated solely from him, engulfed now in the execution of the Tyrant his city and its peoples flew apart, swallowed by his extermination. Korond only did not collapse. He stayed immobile, eyes open wide, lips just parted on one last question. But he was already unanswerably dead.

It was Qo who launched himself at the beast that had wielded the blade. Screeching was Qo, furious with terror and disbelief. Out of Qo's hideous hands extempore magics drizzled.

20

The full moon broke from the earth's rim. Through a slender gap, made only seconds earlier by the implosion of a nearby tower, the enormous disc was clearly visible.

Huth, (the man) apparently was now totally expunged. As always happened at a full moon. He had become his *other* self–a giant lion, tempest-maned and volcano-eyed, had risen up, and it smote Qo with its star-fire talons. They ripped the petty sorcerer end to end. His entrails and conjurings, both, sizzled out. Speechless, down he sprawled.

In a few minutes more almost all of Vay Ezb, and decidedly all of Vay Ezb's citizens, had been extinguished. And at last even the green-eyed palace disintegrated, streaming apart like a slowly shattered window-pane.

Korond's corpse solely stood there, straight and motionless, eyes wide, lips parted, one ineffable hand outstretched as if, once more, to stroke a lion's mane. They say in the Red Hills, and who knows they may be right, he stands there yet, amid the acidulous and smoking shambles of his destructed city. And with the Pretty Knife yet buried in his breast, its diamond point extruded from his spine. But nothing else of him, that is his Tyranny and his cunning power, remain.

The land had been, at a single bound, set free. And like most kept too long in chains, it was groaning and calling as it hugged and stretched itself, howling, sobbing and shouting its thanks to God.

As for Huth, he had sprung up the now cascading devastation of the marble stair, making nothing of that. Over the lunar white-night snowscape, were-lion and successful hero, Huth ran, with the moon at his back and the stars in his teeth, and his soul shined up bright as the morning sun.

The Bench

I sit on the bench, and we fly away.

Nobody else ever seems to come up here. It's where the big old tree grew. They had to cut it down after it was damaged in the storm. Somehow though, on quiet days when I sit on the bench, I still seem to hear the rustle of its leaves, and in autumn, one or two seem to fall past me. But there, the other trees in the park rustle, don't they. And my eyes... well, I'm old. Sometimes one imagines things. Or one's eyes imagine *they* do.

There's a long flight of stone steps that lead up here, from the area with the pools and the flowers. I think the steps put people off. Somebody said to me, once, "Oh, you don't want to climb all the way up there at your age." But they are too stupid to see, of course, at *my* age, it's *exactly* where I *do* want to climb. I want to escape. And up here, with all the chaos and rush, and unkindness and war and horror, and meaningless unreal over-involvement in Nothing, with all that left below and seeming, however self-lyingly, far away, I can be free.

The bench used to stand directly under the tree, but after the lightning struck the tree they cut it down. The bench was all right. They just repainted it. It's the same colour it always was, deep green.

The sun falls here softly through the higher trees across the way. And the trees screen off so much of the park, all the activity, damping down the energetic noise of the football or the loud music or the fights, the conversations, and howling children, that are always being dragged or slapped, never listened to, and all the other arguments. Yes, all that is blotted out. Already you feel far off, and somewhere else.

And then, after a while, I close my eyes.

And then I feel the bench shift a little, only a little. As if it says to me: *Shall we*? Now? *Yes*?

And of course I'm ready. We *shall*. Now.

And up we drift, gentle and strong, into the sky. Upwards, upwards, never a wobble. And through my closed eyelids, the clouds pass by, lit with the sun, misty pale or gold. It's just the way someone once described it to me, when you're in a plane. Except I'm not. I'm sitting on the green bench. And we are flying.

I don't have family. I don't have anyone, you see. But the socially organised people do come round. I find this a bit worrying. I feel like the children who don't get listened to, or if they are, are then put off. I feel I daren't say No. But sometimes I do say it. I can still bathe myself. The shops are very near. One day I suppose I won't be able to manage, and some of these visitors seem to think that day is already here. I'm terrified they'll put me into a hospital, or some dreadful home. I won't even think of that.

Once, about a year ago, I think, after my dog had died, and then the cat, I wanted to replace them. I always took rescued animals and I was always lucky, they were beautiful, and all of them lived, I have to say, to great ages. The cat, for example was almost twenty-one–in cat years over a hundred, much older than I am. But when I thought I'd see if I could get another cat, the social woman advised me not to. "At your age," she said so kindly and tactfully-sadly it was quite brutal and crass, (and just like the one on the steps in the park, too), "it would be difficult for you to cope. And, of course, when–well, when the time comes you might need to go into sheltered accommodation..." I actually think she really meant 'when you drop off the perch, you silly old fool'– "well. Where will the poor cat go then?"

So, I didn't get a cat. Let alone a dog.

But I still climb up the steps to the bench.

I try not to think about death. There's no point, after all. So far as I know, and with the endless medical checks they now demand of you, I guess they must know I'm fairly healthy for my advanced years. So God knows how long I'll go on. Or not.

That polite old man I used to see at the Co-Op, he apparently just dropped dead on the street a week ago, or a couple of weeks, was it? And he was younger than me, I think.

After all there's no choice. Here one day, gone the next. Sometimes I hope there's nothing after death. The idea of an endless dreamless sleep–I don't sleep well any more–seems alluring. And conversely, the notion of a religious Heaven seems exhausting. Or–what do they say?–Astral Plain–where you have to go over all you've done in life and get ready to come back in a new body and put it all right–oh dear. And I wouldn't be *me* anymore. How could I be? So who *would* I be? *What*?

Tonight then, I made a mistake. Just the sort a silly old woman would make, too.

It was a warm and sunny evening–this August has been fine, for a change–and I came to the park and climbed up to the bench and sat down. I thought I'd stay about an hour, get the last sun that filters through low down at that time. Leave the park before sunset, of course. It can get dangerous after that, despite the patrol they've organised. But–well. It's probably the fault of my insomnia. I was so tired, worse than I'd realised. And just relaxing. And when I closed my eyes, and had my waking dream about the bench flying with me up and up–well, I fell asleep.

The first thing I felt when I woke was the darkness. That is, I didn't just *see* it, I felt it on my skin. It was showering down with a dark mist of rain, and far off thunder rumbled.

Storms don't bother me. Not that much does, apart from people. But naturally I thought sensibly I had better get up and go down, and if the gates had been locked, go to the park- keeper's house that backs on to the park, and ask them to let me out, me stammering, no doubt, with embarrassment at my silly-old-foolness.

But just before I moved, the bench made its wonderful kind little shift. As if it says *Shall we*? Now? *Yes*?

And I thought *I mustn't.* But something else that was me, really me, whispered *Yes.* Now. *Yes.*

Exactly then there was this brilliant silver-gold flash like flame. It was so beautiful and lasted several seconds, melting then in a huge purple radiance that seemed to light the sky and the earth end to end. And I felt as I did when I drank my first ever glass of good wine. And as this happened, the bench lifted off and up we went, swimming through the air. And this time I truly saw it all, because my eyes were wide open. Up we flew, through the aura of the trees, through a sort of smoky rainy rainbow, and so into the upper vault of the sky. And the bench seemed–how can I describe this–to be *holding* me–not tight or restrainingly, but the way a nice parent would, a mother or a father, with the child they loved. And everything is–truly *is* changed–

Never before have I ever felt so happy.

I feel so happy now.

It isn't a bench, you see. It's–I don't know what it *is*, but we're flying up and up, up into the stars now. And when we reach the stars–then we'll go on beyond them. It's as if I can remember, although I don't remember. At least, not yet. But I know the bench. I always have.

It was the lightning again, wasn't it? It does strike in the same place twice. And this time it was both of us. But the bench has always known. It carried the tree there, where we're going. And my cats and my dogs, they went there too. And my lover from long ago, the one I did really love. He went there. And now so shall I.

Oh look, the night is opening, just there. Like a sunrise, but it isn't. And the bench isn't a bench. And I'm not–*me*–but I *am*. How wonderful. So I sit on the bench and we fly–away.

Unlocked

Tanith Lee and John Kaiine

I kissed thee ere I kill'd thee, no way but this,
Killing myself to die upon a kiss.
—Shakespeare: Othello

The towers and turrets of St Cailloux, so thin and dark against the terrible sky – I only saw them once. It was not possible to make out the bars, nor to hear the cries. The lawns were shaven, and the trees had the controlled shapes into which they had been carefully cut, restrained by wire. Behind, far off, the mountains, broken and unruly.

Some old chateau, so it looks to be, and must have been, once. No longer.

Now it houses the ones who scream and are kept in by bindings and bars and bolts.

I only saw it once. And that was in a photograph.

When they took me to see the land, they explained all over again, as the lawyer had in the town, that the house was 'lost'.

The land was a shambles too, under that bone-dry sun. Tares and weeds, as in the Bible. And the magnificent old cherry trees, all swarmed with serpents of ivy, although the little apple orchard had no snakes. There could be real snakes underfoot, They warned me. In the black ruin of the house, a glimmer of motion, sun catching something – pale, shimmering.

What a dreadful place. I want only to sell it, although I doubt it will bring in any money.

At the inn, or hotel or whatever it thinks itself to be, an old man brought me a parcel, like a peculiar present.

"What's this?" I tried to be pleasant, though he had suspiciously refused to sit down and ignored my offer of a glass of wine.

"Her book."

"I see. Whose book?"

"Hers. Madame Ysabelle."

"Ah – that's the diary, then."

"Her book," he said, put it on the table, nodded angrily – they are all angry with me, the foreigner from the city who has inherited a piece of their landscape, which is the whole world. The two old servants had been sent away before her death. That is a blessing. I can imagine how *they* would have been with me. "It was found under a stone?" I asked. "By the hearth?"

"What kept it," he said.

After he had gone, I unwrapped the paper and took out the diary. It is black and stained, the binding flaking away. But the stone had protected it, as he said. Something ironic in that, almost a pun—

I opened the cover and saw, in a brownish ink, the characters of my distant relative, Ysabelle, the ornate handwriting so encouraged in her youth. But she had only been thirty-two when she died. No doubt a great age here in the country. An old maid. But I had seen her picture. Quite tall, full-figured, with tight-corseted waist. Hair very dark. Long-fingered hands, and an oval face on a long smooth throat. Dark eyes that gave nothing away, by which I mean *gave* nothing, pushed it toward one.

The writing said, *My Book.* Private, in the manner of a young girl. She had never married, 'Madame', the rude courtesy of this primitive area, never allowed courtship, which was blamed on her father. After his death, alone in her white house, all wood, as they do it here, with only the thinnest veneer of dropping plaster. A grape vine growing over the terrace, and the cherry trees raising their gnarled hag's arms, that in spring are clothed in blossom like a young girl's skin.

By local standards too old then, Ysabelle, for wooing. At twenty, here, they gave up such hopes, unless she was a widow and wealthy, and really, despite the land, the two servants, there was no money in her family.

I flicked through the pages. I did not particularly want to know her. Although her diary had survived, and insistently they had awarded it to me.

Here and there a sentence: "Nightingale in cherry tree. It kept me awake all night. Exquisite song, save when it stops to imitate an owl it has heard in the woods." Or, "Mireio says there are no eggs today." Or, "The wind has been blowing. Has made my head ache and my eyes." Then, this sentence: "I cut open an apple, seeds, the white flesh inside, the juices, white as wine, nobody has witnessed this before."

How odd. What a curious thing to say. Had Ysabelle, who seemed to have gone mad, never supposed anyone, not even Eve, had cut open an apple before?

Then I read, "The red apples all white inside. The leaves are dead, too hot, shrivelling the blooms, too passionate a heat. Bells toll in the next valley. Seeds and tears, poppy dreams. Summer, hot, heat, the stifling heat. I dream of clouds. This brightness hurts me. The silver that the locket is made of – where from? Taken from earth, like blackberries, cherry trees, grapes, peeling birch. Everything will burn. It is holding its last breath, blooming with the threat of death. Foxgloves."

I put the diary down. It had felt hot in my hands. Smoke

rose from it in my imagination.

Walking across to my trunk, I rummaged inside, and pulled out the other thing they had given me; the buckled, shapeless mass of the locket. Why foxgloves, Ysabelle? It must be the old country superstition, not the poison which also gives life, but the black fox – cipher for Satan – who leaves his mark there, because he is the ghost of a lover.

Was her secret here in this diary, then, and did they all know it, all these walnut-brown people of the valleys and slopes, who rose with the sun and slept when it fell, and would tell me nothing, and not even drink a glass of wine with me?

I opened the diary in another place and read, "I saw them today. They were on the road in their little trap with the pony. He sits upright like a stupid rock. She leans, looking this way, that way. Burning hair. Her hair is the sun, but only if the sun is pale as the moon. I waved. And she saw me, and waved too. *He* stared, then nodded, a king. Ernst and Hāna. She had a purple ribbon in her chignon, but her hair is so massive, it drooped on her slender neck, shoulders. Purple like a wound in all that blonde."

Under this, Ysabelle, dimly related to me by the wedlock of an unknown aunt, had drawn a line of vine leaves, rather well, in her brown ink that perhaps had been dark when she used it. Beneath, she writes: "Hāna, Ariadne, Dionysos. Holy."

And then: "Ernst. What a boring statue of shit."

This startles me, and I laugh. *Ysabelle*, such *unfeminine* language. But it is her private book.

Even so, I suddenly think her modern, ahead of her time. This boldness in an old unmarried woman. And she is so coarse about Ernst… does she secretly like him?

The next paragraph only says, "I shall send Jean to advise him about the horse."

I put the diary by my bed. Then, in the furtive manner of this place, pushed it *under the mattress.* I should read more in bed that night.

Arriving back in my room quite early, for they lower their lamps at nine o'clock, and yawn, and shuffle, and frown at you – I sat perversely with the diary, leafing through it, so reluctant to start at the beginning. Surely I shall be bored. What is there here to read? The reflections of an unbalanced, lonely woman, possibly obsessed by her new foreign neighbours, this exciting Ernst made of shit and the woman, his sister, with all that pale hair…

Then something, no, let me be honest, I know precisely what, and it is prurient, ghoulish, makes me turn to the last page. Beyond this page lies the drama of death. The fact that the house of white wood burned, leaving only its hearths and stone floors, and two tall stone chimneys, and Ysabelle's bones, and her diary safe under the hearth stone. Bones and stones. Her neighbours were gone by then, Ernst, Hāna, to their separate places. And by the time of the fire, those who would speak of it had thought Ysabelle mad. The hot weather was not kind to women. The horrible wind that blew from the mountains. The roar of light from their flanks, that had been visible too from the house, and still is from its ground. She had set fire to the house in her craziness, Ysabelle. It was only the kindness of the priest that allowed her Christian burial. She might, after all, have knocked over a lamp. And everything was so dry, flaring up at once—

Was there even a lock on the diary, which the heat from above caused to melt?

Who else has read this book? Who else began by reading the last page first?

"I have a lock of your hair. I cut it from you as you slept. I kissed you there, where the scissors met. You never noticed it had gone. It is all I have of you, your hair. Blonde spirals in a silver locket.

"The locket is cold between my breasts. Cold in the heat. Perhaps it is the heat of the locket that feels cold, as they say witches screamed, when they were burning alive, of the agony of the great terrible freezing coldness. I sweat silver. Your curled hair next to my heart.

"But we are monkeys, not angels.

"Yesterday, when I returned to the old white house, I saw it freshly, as if I had never lived here, or had been away some years. Whose house is that one? Ysabelle's. She lives alone. Truly alone now, for in the town I saw the lawyers, and settled a sum of money on Jean and Mireio. At dawn today, I dismissed them. She was sulky and angry, and he accused me of sending them away because he had tried to shoot the nightingale. Secretly, they were pleased, talking together when they thought I did not hear, of the tobacconist's shop they plan to start together in the next town. Here, a cooking pot and broom are all that remain of them, all they deigned to leave me.

"My new, empty house. I have always liked it. Liked it too well to leave. Nothing has changed since the days of childhood. The peeling painted wooden walls, ivy in the cherry trees – now and then cut back, always returning – the well of broken stone. Such pretty neglect. But yes, the view has changed, the land shrunk and the sky grown. There are no clouds, now.

"I dream of clouds, as indeed I dream of you. Great black clouds to cover the sun, stormy skies to quell this heat. There has been no rain for many months, and I have heard a rumour too, of a goat sacrificed in the woods – killing to bring rain, blood for water.

"I have a lock of your hair. And *this*. I have this, but this is not you. No. How well I remember when it was. For it was the very same height as you, and broader perhaps, than your delicate, slender frame, like a spilling of your soul in silver. How we sat, night after night, brushing your hair, this entity of you, combing it out, both of us marvelling, for I *made* you marvel at the wonder of it that you had never seen it was. Combing, braiding, playing, plaiting with ribbons, silks, the nights you wore it loose, for me, around you like – a shroud. Oh, Hāna. Your hair.

"I have made it into a noose, threaded, sewn with faded mauve. A noose is all now it is worthy to be, this, that was your wedding train. Life, that will be death.

"They call the asylum also the Valley of Wolves – St Stones, St Cailloux. A sort of pun. And this is, too, for I shall put it under the stone of the hearth, and who knows who will ever find it, my Book. But I hope they will, for I want them to know, yes, even if they rage and curse, I want them to know of you. And that my last thought will be of you, dying on a kiss. Good night, Hāna."

For weeks, the valley and the village were alive with gossip concerning the strangers, who were strange in all ways – educated, and not badly off, from another planet – that is, another country – and unrelated even in the faintest sense, to anyone of the locality.

The village people spied on the newcomers, and presently told each other that here was Madame Ysabelle's chance. For the foreign householder, Monsieur Ernst, was unwed, not poor, nor very young, and of the same social class as Madame Ysabelle, who after all, was not bad-looking, and had her land, if only she would bother to see it worked. The single potential stumbling block might be Monsieur Ernst's sister, also unmarried, who lived with and looked after her scholarly brother, in just the same way as Ysabelle had looked after her scholarly father until his death, three years before. The sister was old, so the spies decided, who had only seen her from a distance. She had white hair. These females were often the very worst, and the evidence suggested she must have kept him from union before.

The two houses, though, were only half an hour's walk from each other. One day or another, the man and the woman must meet.

It was a fact, there were dual elements in the village, indeed in all the villages and farms of the region. A sort of peasant bourgeoisie existed; gossipy, religious, caste-conscious, exacting. But, too, there was the more feral peasant blood, which had other values, and was considered little better than a pack of wild beasts. These latter had actually troubled properly to see *Mademoiselle* Hāna – she was yet young enough for that, twenty-four years, which to them looked nineteen. Two men had carried boxes to the house of Monsieur Ernst. A woman had brought eggs, and later come to see to the washing. These people knew quite soon that it was the brother who was the stiff one. If he had not married, it was because he had never seen a woman he liked sufficiently. And his sister gave him the best of care – she was what the middle shelf of the region would have termed *devoted.* To the 'wild beasts', perhaps, she was dutiful, and this while she was not the sort of girl who would be naturally constrained. She too had vestiges of the wild woods, where once witches had danced with flowers in their hair, just as they had ridden from the mountains on their broomsticks not thirteen years before.

Of Ysabelle also this wild quality might have been noted, in her girlhood. They had seen her, wandering the fields with blood-red poppies in her basket. Or watching the moon from her window while her clever father pored over his books.

To the Wild Beasts, Hāna did not represent an obstacle nor Ernst a rescue. Although they were not insensible to ideas of rescue and obstacle in the arrival of the foreign couple.

Ysabelle met Ernst one morning. He was riding along the lane, or road, that ran by the wall of the garden at the front of her house, and she was standing there with Mireio, over the scattered feathers of a chicken some fox had taken in the night.

Mireio was cursing the fox, and promising that Jean would set a trap, and Ysabelle impatiently was desiring that rather than do this, the house of the chickens should be repaired.

They argued in the way old servant women did with mistresses they had known as children, and youngish mistresses with old servant women who had almost been their mothers, but were not.

Ernst stopped the trap, and frankly watched, in cool amusement.

When Ysabelle looked, he raised his hat and introduced himself.

Doubtless he could see the old servant eyeing him, evaluating him, but with Ysabelle there was none of that. As he had heard, she was educated and well-bred, and he liked the look of her, her coal-black hair softly but neatly dressed, her dark dress, still in part-mourning apparently, for an adored, respected father. Her lush figure, too, her graceful features, her sensitive, noble hands.

She answered him politely.

Ernst said, with his perfect command of language and dialect, "I hope my sister may come over and visit you? Of course, there's no one else suitable for her to see, for miles. She's an absolute angel to me. I want her to be happy, but how can a woman be happy with no other women sometimes to chatter to?"

Ysabelle dipped her raven-coloured eyes. She did not smile. As she was doing this, Mireio said, aggressively, "There is the duck, Madame. I said it was too much for us. But for a proper supper for three, it would be perfect."

Ernst let out a roar of laughter. This was as good as a comedy at the theatre, and really he had no objection to sitting over a good country meal, and looking at Ysabelle, and watching her come around to him. "Well, I should be honoured," he said, "but Madame hasn't yet asked me."

Ysabelle glanced at him. No smile. Quiet as silence. She said, however, "Mireio has decided you must taste her cooking. Please come and taste it."

They agreed an evening, and Ernst rattled away to the town, whistling, and that night told his sister they were to meet a true witch of a woman, who, he was sure, had already laid a spell on him, because he was going to take with them a bottle of his best wine.

"When I first saw you tonight, with the sun just down and the moon just risen, I was so angry and nervous. The stupid supper. Not since my father had I had to suffer in that way. When he died, the freedom gave me wings. And now, I should be trapped, as Jean wished to trap the poor fox, gnawing through my paws to get away. Seeing you, I hated you. You. One entire second, that I will never forget or forgive. I hated your freshness, your glow, your light-coloured hair, your face, eager to be liked, and nervous too, I am sure. Hated you. I punished myself later, when you were gone. I went upstairs and said to myself in the mirror, *you hated her.* And I slapped my own face, hard, and left a red mark that lasted two hours. I know, I was awake so long."

Ernst made the meal 'go', talking all the while, a sort of lecture. He was studying many things, philosophical, medical, and had also an interest in fossils, many examples of which he would find, he said, in the local countryside, for it was rich in them. Hāna, of course, did not understand these interests. "She calls me to task, and says I march about all day, obsessed by stones. Stones, Madame Ysabelle. I ask you."

Ysabelle looked at Hāna, and Hāna said, softly, with her slight accent, her slight, always half-stumbling in the new language, "Oh, but I know they're – wonderful, Ernst. I do. I only wish I could have seen them – when they were alive.

The big animals like dragons, and the little insects."

"She is a tyrant. She also insists archaeology is tomb robbery," said Ernst.

Ysabelle said, "Mademoiselle Hāna would prefer to travel in time."

"Yes," said Hāna, "to go back and see it as it was."

"She reads that sort of nonsense," he said.

Ysabelle said, "But monsieur, you know what we women are. Creatures of feeling, not intellect."

"That takes a clever woman to say," gallantly declared Ernst. He added, "Of course, I've heard of your father. I read a book of his. An excellent mind."

"Thank you. He was much admired."

"You must miss him."

"Yes," she said, "every day."

And turning, as Ernst applied himself again to the duck, Ysabelle saw Hāna stare at her almost with a look of fear.

Later Ysabelle took Hāna to inspect the garden, to show her womanly things, domestic herbs, the husbandry of the grapevine, the moon above a certain tree.

Hāna said abruptly, "You take a risk, Madame."

"Oh? In what way?"

"Making fun of him. He has a horrible temper."

"Yes, I'm sure that he does."

"He doesn't see it now, what you're doing—"

"I'll be more careful."

"Please. Because I'd hate there to be a rift."

"Since you have no other female companions."

"Of course I do," said Hāna. "There are lots of woman here I like very well. He's often away on his business, things to do with his money, and clever papers he's written. Then I sit on the wall of the court with the servant girl, shelling peas, giggling. We take off our shoes."

"I'm sure that is a risk, too."

Hāna said nothing. Then she said, "We've been to many places. I like this valley." Though her delivery was still hesitant, it was now a fluent, unafraid hesitancy.

The moon stood in the top of the birch, which held it like a white mask upon feathers.

Hāna lifted her face. She was so pale, her white skin and lightly-tinted mouth. Her eyes were dark, although not so dark as Ysabelle's. As Hāna tipped back her head, Ysabelle, who had drunk Ernst's very strong wine, had a momentary irrational fear that the incredible weight of Hāna's chignon would pull back and dislocate her slender neck. And throwing out one hand, she caught the back of Hāna's head in her palm, as a woman does with a young child or baby.

Hāna said nothing, resting her head, so heavy, the massy cushion of silken hair, on Ysabelle's hand.

They gazed up at the moon, at the mask which hid the moon, which might itself in reality be a thing of darkness, concealing itself for ever from the earth.

"I've never seen so much hair," said Ysabelle presently.

"Yes, it makes my head ache sometimes. I wanted to cut some of it once. But Ernst told me that was unfeminine."

"What nonsense. Your brother's a fool. I'm sorry. Even so, you shouldn't – no, you should never cut your hair. Your hair isn't like any other hair. Your hair is – *you.*"

Hāna laughed.

Ysabelle in turn felt frightened. She said, "What nonsense *I'm* talking." And took the girl back into the house, which Ernst was filling, as the father had done, with the headachy lustre of cigars.

They left at midnight, a city hour, not valued in the country.

Exhausted, Ysabelle went upstairs, and Mireio, hearing her pace about, nodded sagely, rightly believing her mistress was disturbed by new and awful terrors, tinglings, awakenings, amazements.

Ernst was delighted when Hāna began to spend time with Ysabelle at the white wooden house, among the cherries. She was always returned early enough to greet him, if he had been absent in the town. She made sure as ever that the servants saw to his comforts. When once or twice he slyly said to Hāna, "What do you talk about, you two women, all those hours? Daydreams, and those books of yours, I expect."

Hāna replied seriously, "Sometimes we talk about you."

"Me? What place can a humble male have in your games?" But he needed no answer and was gratified, not surprised, by Hāna's lie. She had learned to be careful of him from an immature age, upbraiding him only in the proper, respectful, foolish, feminine way, desisting at once when chided. She was used to extolling his virtues, praising his achievements and being in awe of them. Even her perhaps-feigned loyalty she had learned to temper, for once, when a rival at his university had, he said, stolen a passage from his paper, and Hāna had asserted that the man should be whipped, Ernst had replied sharply that this might be so, but he did not expect *her* to say it. Hāna had been taught that men were not to be questioned, save by other men. For though some men were base, a woman could not grasp what drove them to it.

All this Hāna had relayed to Ysabelle, it was true. And so, in a way, they *had* spoken of Ernst.

"My mother died when I was four," said Hāna, "but I had a kind nurse. I miss my mother still, do you know, I dream of her even now. She'd come in from some ball or dinner and her skirts would rustle, and she smelled of perfume, and there was powder on her cheek, as on the wings of the butterflies that Ernst kills."

"I killed my mother," said Ysabelle. Hāna gazed, and Ysabelle added, "I mean, when I was born. Of course, as I grew, I had to take her place in many ways, for my father. For other consolations, he went to the town."

Hāna lowered her eyes. They were a deep shadowy brown, like pools in the wood where animals stole to slake their thirst.

They walked about the countryside, the two women. They picked flowers and wild herbs and, later, mushrooms. They talked the sort of talk that Ernst would have predicted. Of memory and thought and feeling and incoherent longings. They sometimes laughed until their waists, held firm in the bones of dead whales, ached. They read books together aloud. Even, they shelled peas and chopped onions on the broad table, Mireio scolding them as if they were children. She would spoil it soon enough, saying, "Monsieur must come tomorrow or next day. This pork will just suit him." She was ready always with her invitations to Ernst, was Mireio, and he eager to accept them.

Ysabelle, he remarked to himself, *has that woman very well primed*. He did not mind a little connivance, though, aimed at himself. Ysabelle herself would not be too forward, and she would not anticipate, daughter of a free-thinking intellectual as she was, anything he did not want to give.

But too, she must be parched, surrounded by the local males, such swinish illiterates. How she must look forward to the sound of *his* step, *his* voice, after all that girlish twittering. And she had a lovely bosom; he had seen the white upper curves of it in her once-fashionable, country evening gown, and her firm white arms. Her hair smelled of the rose-essence with which she rinsed it. And there was the smell of cherries always in the house now, somehow inciting. He would like to take a bite, there was no denying it.

"He'll be gone – oh, two nights, three. He said, I might ask you to stay with me."

"Did he."

"Have I offended? – I hoped – you see, when he's not there, you've no idea, Ysabelle, our maid, Gittel, is so funny—"

"I prefer not to leave my house. But you're welcome to stay with *me*. I'm afraid—" Ysabelle hesitated. She paled, which, in the candlelight, hardly showed, "we would have to share the bed. The other rooms aren't properly cared for. But this bed is very large. It was my mother's when my father – you understand. A large, ample couch. It's strange. My servants are going away too. A visit I promised them. Gone for two nights. But we would manage, wouldn't we?"

Hāna's face. An angel announcing peace to all the world. "But I wouldn't – annoy you?"

Now Ysabelle, stumbling with a familiar language, her own. "Annoy – I – enjoy your company so much."

"I remember my mother," Hāna said, "before she died. Late, she'd wake me. She used to give me sweets, and play with me, all sorts of silly games, how we laughed. And she'd hold me in her arms. She said, 'We are two little mice, my love. When the cat's from home, the mice will dance'."

"Wine and opium. A dream of pearls. Hidden things. Clasp. Hinges. Unhinged. Open. The quiet shout, my cherry blossom. How we sat, that night. And you loosed your hair. My pearl, shut away, the hair in the locket – your little river – my river in the time of drought. The making of your sweet rain. My souvenir. A wedding train, it swept to the floor. Tread on my heart and break it. Your arms – flung up in abandon, your impatient body, waiting. You had fallen asleep, your face hidden in hair, your legs pale, ghostly in the candlelight. I drew nearer, and the candle with me, flickering, threw shadows dancing between your thighs. I grew jealous of light. I inhaled you there, breathed you in. Kissed you and kissed you again, bathed in the little rivers of you. The heat of the candle was stifling, agonising. We blew the flame away with our mouths. We embraced darkness, drank the night. Oh, Hāna. Hāna, Hāna."

Hāna was at the door in the stillness of the hot evening. The nightingale was already singing, and the sun hung low, the sky a choked pastel blue, as in a faded painting.

On the terrace, Hāna paused. "May I step over?"

Ysabelle laughed. She was unsettled, vivid and anxious. "Like the ghost? If I ask you in, will you haunt me?"

"No, I shall be circumspect."

"Come in. Haunt my house."

The rooms smelled of the absence of things. The absence of the servants, gone to their family of a hundred nieces and grandsons in the town. The absence of cooking. It was very hot, and the wooden parts of the building creaked. Ysabelle had lit a lamp in her sitting room, and another in the kitchen, and the strings of onions glowed like red metal. In a vase stood three white flowers. She poured from the bottle of wine. They drank. And Hāna came and kissed her, a fleeting little trustful kiss, at the corner of the mouth.

"Such fun," said Hāna.

"Oh, my child," said Ysabelle, and a well of sadness was filled.

"No. We're sisters. My mother is your mother. And Ernst—"

"Ernst," said Ysabelle, looking into her glass.

"Ernst never was born," said Hāna. And her face was wicked, pitiless. "It was you. We two. You can be the clever one. And I'll look after you."

"I'm not clever."

"Yes."

The light was darkness. The sky a blue jewel in every narrow window. The nightingale sang a thousand and one songs, like Scheherazade, never repeating itself.

They made an omelette with fresh herbs and mushrooms, and ate two loaves of the coarse good bread. They opened another bottle, and made the coffee, which had come from the town, seething it like soup, and adding cream and cognac.

They talked. Whatever do women talk of? Such nonsense. Of life and death, of the soul, of the worlds hidden behind the woods, the mountains, the sky, the ground. Of

God, of – love.

"Did you never love anyone?" asked Hāna.

"No."

"Your – father."

"How could I love him? He simply always inexorably was, like the year, the day. An hour. An hour without end. Do you love your brother?"

"I – feel sorry for him."

Ysabelle – laughed. A new laugh. Bitter? Stern?

"But he can do anything," said Ysabelle.

"He – does not – *see*," said Hāna. "He breaks the stone, and the fossil is there. But he sees only this. Not what it was. Its life. And medicine – experiments – he has done things with small animals – and there is a horrible man he consorts with, a sort of doctor. And the butterflies on pins. Their patterns. But not – not what they are. He doesn't see God."

"Do you?"

"Oh yes," said Hāna, simply, quiet, a truthful child.

"Then what does God seem to be?"

"Everything. All things."

"A man. A king. A lord."

"No," said Hāna. She smiled. "Nothing like that."

When they went up to bed, dousing the lamps, carrying the fat white candle, their bodies moved up the stairs as if all matter had been freshly invented. Night, for example. The stars between the shutters. The cry of the fox from far away. The far shapes of the mountains on the dark. The dark. The furniture. Clothes. Bodies. Skin.

"Will you take down your hair?"

"Yes. Then I'll plait it. There's such a lot. I'll tie it up close so it won't trouble you."

Ysabelle said, "May I watch you?"

In the candlelight, Hāna, a portrait, pale as alabaster, and gems of gold in her eyes. "Oh *yes*. I used to watch my mother."

In the old story, the basket issues ropes of silver, and the silver flows on. Or the silver water leaps from the rock, and never stops.

Pins came out, and combs. The two ribbons were undone. Hāna, unwinding from her head the streams of the moon. On and on. Flowing. Never stopping.

The hair poured, and fell, and fell, and hung against the floor, just curling over there. A heavenly veil.

"Oh Hāna," said Ysabelle. "Your hair."

"Too much."

"No. Don't plait it – *don't*. Haven't you ever known?"

Under the sheath of hair, so simple to undress unseen. The train of an empress, when seated, spreading in folds. Standing again, veiled in the moon, she climbs into the wide bed. But lying back, the sea of moonlight parts.

"I'm so sleepy," says Hāna. She yawns. She starts to speak, and sleeps.

Her upturned breast. What is it like? So soft, so kind, like a white bird, sleeping. And her hollow belly, and her thighs. And the mass of her silver hair, even in her groin, thick and rich and pale as fleece. The scent of her which is thyme and lilies – and – something which *lives*, and is warm.

Ysabelle stands. Locked. Her clasped hands under her chin. The voiceless weeping runs down her face as hot as blood.

But where the candle falls. Is it possible that you can steal a kiss, and not wake Beauty?

"Please – forgive me—"

"But it's so lovely. Don't stop—"

"I can't—"

The nightingale sings. Hāna – sings.

"I never—"

"But you must have—"

"No. What is it? Oh – so wonderful—"

"You don't hate me—"

"I love you. Is it possible – could it happen again?"

"Yes."

"And for you?"

"Oh, yes, for me. Touch – there. Can you tell?"

"But – it's like the fountain in The Bible, springing forth. I used to think that must be tears. But it's this—"

"Hāna—"

"You're so dark. Oh, I love you. I can see you in the dark. Blow out the light."

Blow out the light... Put out the light... *I kiss'd thee ere I kill'd thee.*

He was pleased that evidently they had had a nice time together. He liked them to get on. He questioned his sister, trying to elicit some news of what had been said – of him. Hāna hinted a little, only that. Sly thing. He could picture it, these women, and Ysabelle sighing over him, and Hāna telling foolish stories admiringly, secretively, the way women did. His university glories, his boyish foibles, his favourite toy – they had that look now, of confidences exchanged.

It was afternoon, and Ysabelle and Hāna sat in the sitting-room of Ernst's house on the slope.

They were rather stiff and upright, as Ernst was. They drank a tisane, and looked at the view, for soon he would arrive home from his fossil hunt along the edge of the mountains.

The mountains loomed here. At the white house, on such a hot day, they were more a presence of burning light in the windows. Mireio had, as she always did in summer, moved two or three pictures in glass away from the reflection – some superstition that Ysabelle had never questioned, in all her thirty-two years.

But the mountains were oppressive, in this other spot They turned the sun off in one direction, and cast a sort of shade.

Ysabelle said softly, "If I had you alone, heaven knows what I'd do to you."

"How startled I should be."

"I'd nibble at you like a lettuce."

"If only you could."

They saw him on the path, dwarfed by distance, tiny, big and towering, sunburnt, carrying some trophy.

They turned into two whale bones; corseted tight, dead and hard and upright.

He entered. The door slammed, and the servant girl, Gittel, ran up – noise, fluster – and then he was in the room, enormous, and he must be welcomed and begged to tell his wishes. Send Gittel to heat the kettle, the coffee must be prepared. And look, here were the almond cakes bought especially, as he liked them, and some pâté that had been kept untouched and cool in the stone larder.

Would he sit? No. Was he tired? No. But surely, he must be tired a little, after so long an excursion? No. One saw how he watched, amused, the fuss. How strong and brave he was, to have walked so long and still be walking about, and to have broken this rock, which now he put down on the table there. How astonishing. How erudite he was, to have found it. To have known where.

He spread the broken halves and showed the fossil, the little images, turned to stones, curling and perfect, ammonites, molluscs, from a sea long gone, in this afternoon of drought.

"Look here."

They clustered for the lesson. So impressed by him, gasping.

"Nobody has witnessed this before," he said.

It was true. They could not argue with him.

Later, alone a moment, she cut the apple, showed it to Hāna. "Nobody," said Ysabelle, "has witnessed this before."

"But it's only an apple. Many people—"

"Not *this* apple. Nobody, save you and I, have witnessed

the inside of *this* apple, before."

"Oh Ysabelle. You're too clever – I'm afraid—"

"Yes, yes, my darling. So am I."

This is Ernst's house. Against the shadow mountains.

In the evening, after the thick soup and the cheese and wine, his cigars, and looking at the brown mass settling on the sides of the heights. Darkness will come. Cannot be held back. Nobody has witnessed this before, not *this* night.

"Oh, my good friend, yes, Le Ruc. Of course, he has his life's work at St Cailloux. A genius," said Ernst, who had made the evening 'go', speaking, entertaining them, and even, in the case of Ysabelle, perhaps able to teach her somewhat. She was promising, Ysabelle. She might write up his notes for the paper on ammonites of the region. A fine clear hand. Her father was to be congratulated posthumously. "I've mentioned, he's fascinated, Le Ruc, by the surgical procedures of Ancient Egypt. But also of course by the most modern inventions. The X-ray now, what a wonder."

"Seeing inside," Hāna said after, another moment alone, "Nothing is to be private."

But Ernst said, "We can't pretend to be delicate. We're monkeys, not angels. Descended from the apes. Not even *you* are an angel, Ysabelle." He raised his glass. "So your appearance must be deceptive."

"Ernst telling us," Ysabelle, writing later, in her clear hand, "with such costive glee, of a machine, which can see the very bones *inside* a body. Nothing is left secret. And the fossils, asleep for centuries. What a pillager he is, raping his way over the foothills."

Taken home, in the trap. Ernst had insisted. Hāna left behind. Ernst. The moon high. They have sacrificed a goat in the woods for rain. The blood has splashed the moon. There are marks on it.

"Ysabelle."

She sits silent, listening. At last she says, "Ernst – you

flatter me. But – you frighten me, Ernst. I've never known a man so – powerful – so very *wise*. Even my father."

"Ysabelle, don't be afraid of me. What has my intellect to do with this? You inflame me, Ysabelle."

"No, Ernst. I'm unworthy of you. I couldn't bring myself – you'd be disappointed – how could I bear that? You would come to despise me. Oh, ten years ago, perhaps. Not now."

"Don't suppose, Ysabelle, I'm done with you. I shan't give up."

"Please. My dear friend. You must."

"One kiss."

"No, Ernst I must be firm. What would you think if I had no honour?"

In the house of white-painted wood, retching into the iron sink, spitting the bitter bile, his wine.

He is tickled now. Soon he will be disillusioned.

"Hāna, can't we fly away on the white angel wings of your hair?"

Ernst's house stands there, at the top of the valley. It is well-maintained and there are many rooms. In the courtyard, the well has sweet water, which has almost run dry. It was once, this house, the domicile of a rich aristocrat. But that was long ago, before men learned they were descended from monkeys.

Shutters hang by the windows, the colour the mountains become in the sinking heat of evening.

Ysabelle looks at this house. Now she is often here. *He* has insisted. She must stay here, tonight. *He* must be the dominant one, not Ysabelle, who is a woman. There are more comforts here. And Hāna need not travel.

Ysabelle does not like the house. It seems to her, everything is held inside this building, confined. Just as the land confines the valley. The clouds confine the rain.

But they – can make rain.

In the midst of arid dry compression, the spring leaps forth. Oh, yes, even once when he was below, doing one of the things he does, something with knives or pins, pushing him from thought, in the upper room, clinging, and that enough—

But tonight, in the hot-brown, baked-closed-shutness of the house. For the cat is away. The cat is away again for one more night.

"Let us dance. I walked here, dancing. Never before has anyone witnessed the cream of your thighs, the fleece of silver-gold – I cut a curl, two, three, from this sacred place, as you slept, and the god slept inside you. I – robbed you – did I? Did I? No, not robbery. Only too shy to say. One day I will confess, show you. Ysabelle that you call clever. I clipped the little curls and put them in this locket of silver, snapping shut the face of it upon my souvenir. Its hinges... Unhinged.

"I have a lock of your hair in my locket, cold between my breasts, or is it boiling hot? I cut the curls so carefully I did not even wake you. Your gardens – your sweet breasts, small as a girl's, your perfect face in its wreathes of angel wings. The centre of your life, your womb, behind its treasury silver-golden gate, soft as ermine."

The house is watching, as Ysabelle climbs towards it, but she thinks that is only Hāna, watching from the upstairs window, where she has strewn perfume in the bed.

"Night after night you loosed your hair. That greater river – dry, yet feeling wet to my thirst. But here there is no smell of cherries ripening. This house of his smells masculine, except for the sanctuary of your room, with the wild flowers in the vase, and the chocolate standing in its pot. You are my cherry-fruit."

"He went to that awful – to the asylum."

"St Cailloux? St Stones..."

"That man – Le Ruc – Ernst is intrigued by the – what does he say? – the *so-interesting* patients. By the operations Le Ruc discusses with him and wants to carry out. These disgusting things he says the physicians of the pharaohs did—"

"Why are you talking of *him*?"

"I don't know."

"It's because we are here. Tomorrow, after he comes back – make some excuse... I know, I shall forget my basket. Then you must bring it to me. Such a womanly thing. How can I manage without it?"

"He'll say I should send Gittel."

"*Bring* Gittel. She and Mireio love gossiping."

"Perhaps. He's irritable. He calls you *Juno*. What is that?"

"The wife of the king of the gods in Ancient Rome. She was frosty, sour. A nag – that dreadful thing women do because men won't listen."

"Then he's asked you for favours?"

"Oh—"

"And you put him off. Ysabelle!"

"What? Do you want me to say yes?"

"No – *no* – but he's so proud—"

"He's a monster. He'll grow tired of hunting me."

"He has begun to dislike you. Tonight he said to me, *Be careful what you say to her.*"

"Then – I must flatter him more. Oh God," said Ysabelle, "I'd even accept his caresses, if it were the only way."

They sat in silence. Why was the silence so strange? Of course, here there was no nightingale.

"Perhaps," said Ysabelle, "I can contrive to put some stupid petty woman in his way, one that won't recoil."

"Sometimes ..." said Hāna, "when I was only ten, I had

little breasts, and he tried and tried to see them. When I wouldn't, he made up a story about me to our father. I don't know what Ernst said, but my father had my nurse tie my hands together every night for three months. She used to cry as she did it. But she'd never explain."

Ysabelle got up. Before she could prevent herself, she retched violently. Hāna rushed to her. At the touch of Hāna the sickness was gone.

"Dionysos," said Ysabelle, "the god of wine and madness, the breaker of chains – do you see sometimes, in the woods, the pine cones piled up together into the form of another cone, the drawing of an eye on a tree or rock? – that's the Eye of the Mother, whom Dionysos sometimes represents. And they killed two goats, and they poured wine. Let's run away, Hāna."

"How can we?" said Hāna.

It was true. They were immovable, fixed. One to the man, his life. The other to a place. They did not properly see this, how they had been warped to fit and nailed home. And yet escape was closed by a deep invisible wall.

Ysabelle thought, *Perhaps he'll die. An accident, thrown from the trap as the pony bolts at a flash of lightning, a clap of moistureless thunder from the mountains. Or too much drink, a haemorrhage.*

But Hāna kisses her breasts and Ysabelle melts like wax, and flows down into the rose-red fire.

Their clothes thrown away, murmuring in the stillness, cries choked back, not even a nightingale to shield them with her noisy song.

Hinges. Unhinged.

A locket? A door? Madness?

The story, told locally, clandestinely, was that Ernst returned unexpectedly, after all, that night – perhaps a quarrel with his friend? The house was in darkness and silence, and so he went up quietly to bed, which does not seem very like him. One would imagine actually he would make a disturbance, rouse everyone up, want things done. Or could he have been suspicious?

Passing – on tiptoe? Surely not – the door to Hāna's room, he heard them whispering, and the creak of the wooden bed.

He flung the door wide on its hinges and found them naked, hair down, uncorseted, undone – his sister Hāna and Madame Ysabelle.

This is not the case.

Ernst rode home in the trap at about nine in the morning from his country breakfast with Le Ruc. There had been no quarrel, for Ernst and Le Ruc enjoyed a perfect mutual respect and approbation, tinctured pleasantly for each by a wisp of well-concealed tolerance; Le Ruc for Ernst's slight blindness to the essentials of science, since Ernst was so bound up in theory, nature and the world; Ernst for Le Ruc's slight blindness to theory, nature and the world, since Le Ruc was absorbed utterly by science.

Ernst was not in an ill mood. Only the idea of Ysabelle having stayed with his sister that night was a small but tart irritant, that had begun to work on him directly he brought the trap on to the rough road, and saw her house before him under the mountains.

Ysabelle was a tease, or a fool. He was beginning, frankly, to notice the failings she had pointed out to him in herself, the elements that made her, she said, unworthy of him. Her 'fear' of him he was not, now, so certain of. For fear, to women, was of course a powerful aphrodisiac. It had seemed to him, some four days previously, that this might be the real fount of her desires – to be physically mastered. And so, entering her home on the pretext of requiring eggs from Mireio's hens, he had ended by pressing Ysabelle harshly to the wall of her white wooden sitting-room, brutally kissing her mouth, penetrating it with his tongue, while with his free hand he mounded her skirt and squeezed, through layers of clothing, her most interesting feature.

She had somehow got away from him, and stood panting, her face as white as a china plate, her eyes inflamed. This might be arousal, and he approached her again, at which she hoarsely said, "I won't be responsible for any harm." And pulled a fire-iron up from the stone hearth.

"If you keep on like this," he said, "you'll put me off."

"Get away from me," she cried, like a peasant. But then she shook herself and said, putting down the nasty-looking implement, "Excuse me, Ernst. But I'm not for you. I can't – expose myself to the tragedy of losing you, once you tire of me. You know how women are. This sort of liaison – will mean so much more to me."

"I'd think, from another woman, this was a demand for a bourgeois marriage."

Ysabelle threw back her head and laughed. She was hysterical and unappealing. Women were unhinged, one knew this, at certain times more so, and she was approaching that age when they were at their worst.

Why had he fancied her? Well, this was a barren spot.

He himself laughed shortly. "Then, good morning."

Outside, Mireio came sidling with a basket of eggs. It seemed to him she leered at his reddened mouth. Doubtless that other bitch thought she could get more out of him by frustrating him, but he was not of that sort. Besides, if ever he were to marry, he would want youth, for sons, and some money, too.

His annoyance with Ysabelle did not abate as, mentally, he cast her off. He supposed this was a sexual matter. She had led him on, now would not accommodate him as she had hinted she would.

He did not like her. No. He would rather she did not come any more into his house. And Hāna must be warned. Hāna was too trusting, and such women as Ysabelle were not to be trusted. Particularly by their own sex, for women were faithless, and nowhere more so than with each other, filling each other's heads with idiocy, always jealous, treacherous.

Seeing presently his own country house from the trap, Ernst thought that perhaps they might go back to the city. Le Ruc could be invited to stay there, in a proper flat, say, with amenities, and efficient servants. Or perhaps not, for Hāna might well make eyes at him, as she had done before with their few male visitors, afterwards making out they had frightened her – familiar tale!

Some way still from Ernst's house, the pony, unsatisfactorily also his property, cast a shoe.

Ernst got out, and stood cursing, damning the beast. Then he left it there, and went on foot towards his home, where Gittel must be sent to fetch a man for the horse from the village.

So, he approached, walking, in a morning loud with bird song – even the nightingales that, here, had not used their voices through the night A church bell was tolling too, in the next valley. This was for a burial.

He saw them in a little nook, between the wall and a leaning wild cedar. Hāna's hair was partly unpinned, but Ysabelle was dressed for her journey home along the upper valley. She wore her dark gown, as usual. She looked quite conventional, and conceivably, if he had met her like this, returning from the visit, as he would have done, a minute later, he would have thought her in fact very plain, of very little importance to himself.

But now she moved to his sister Hāna, and concealed yet not concealed, down on the road, unannounced by the wheels of the trap and the pony's homecoming trot, he watched them. He saw how they grew together, breast to breast, their arms around each other's necks, thigh to thigh, lip to lip. They were an image and an image in a mirror, clasped.

Really, it was not much. Women kissed. Friends might kiss. And yet, this *passion*. Smoke rose from their skins, the air about them trembled, as later in the day the heat of the drought would make it do.

Ernst ran. He ran straight at them. They heard him then, his gallop over the track, his blundering rush across the little scattered stones, and the dust rose round him. He was a whirlwind. He thrust them apart as they were themselves thrusting apart. Ysabelle fell back into the bole of the tree, slipped down it, sat in the dust, staring. Hāna he slapped, once, twice, across her face.

He was roaring, like a lion, like a bull—

His words – were there any words? Oh yes, jargon of streets and alleys, epithets old as humankind. But words? Were there any? Are there any, for such rage?

Hāna attempted to speak. He raised his hand to strike her again and Ysabelle, staggering up, caught his arm, hung on it, and so he flung her off, sprawling again, and this time heard her thin, quick cry of pain.

Now language assembled itself. Not whores – madwomen. They were mad. Their brains – diseased.

He swept up Hāna and bore her off. Suddenly, it was so very visible, the differences in their size and strength, as if he and she were beings of two unlike species.

Her arms outstretched, she called to Ysabelle – "No, don't try to stop him—"

And Ysabelle, her knee twisted by the violence of her fall to boneless water, could only lie on her side, as if indolent, observing this, observing Hāna borne along in a cloud of dust and hair, into the brown masculine house that smelled of maleness and cigars. While another cloud, purple as Hāna's ribbons, covered the screech of the sun.

Ysabelle walked home. That is, she limped, crawled. She fainted three times, the pain was so great. Finally, she dropped on the road before her own house, and Mireio, who saw it, brought Jean, who carried Ysabelle inside. Thus, both women were carried into a house by a man, and helpless.

"I fell, and twisted my leg."

This was exact if not decorous. Or true.

As she lay on her bed, her knee packed with the poultices of herbs, tightly bound, and beating like a drum, sometimes leaning to vomit in a chamber-pot, Ysabelle turned over in her mind what she should do. But she was feverish, and could not be sure what had happened. How could Ernst have deduced, from their parting embrace, so much? Yet he had. Indeed, it could not be denied. Of course, any woman who rejected him must be – unnatural. Already condemned. Hopeless.

She would have gone to his door, limping, crawling, but the girl, Gittel, had run out. Gittel, terrified, heaving Ysabelle up and bending under her weight like a young willow. Her thick accent: "Go – go, Madame. She'll calm him. She always does, the four years I'm with them."

And Gittel had pushed Ysabelle away. And from the male house, no sound issued. The birds sang on. The clouds passed intermittently across the sun. Eclipses.

It was Ysabelle he would condemn. She was a witch who had seduced—

Hāna, so ignorant, naive, unable to judge, to see the deadly snare—

He would reprimand and instruct. He might be cruel. He might strike her again, and lock her up in her room. Then he would come here. Ysabelle, her brain white with the lights that splashed over her eyes, formulated what she must do. "Oh Ernst – Ernst – after our last time together – I thought you loathed me. Don't you know how women sometimes *pretend* – so foolish – she let me, out of pity – she let me make-believe – that she was *you*!"

And then, stroking him, begging him to take her, his stinking filthy body, his disgusting tongue, and worse, the rest – the rest. But Ysabelle would have it all, she would do anything. For that way, she could protect – she would even take his member, as she had heard tell a prostitute – a *mad* prostitute presumably – would do, take it into her mouth –

and choking down her revulsion, moaning as if with joy, become his utter slave.

She would die for him, if she must.

Hāna…

Mireio said to Jean that she thought that bad man, Monsieur Ernst, had led Ysabelle a dance, and cast her off. No matter. If there was a pregnancy, it could he dealt with... Mireio was skilled. But after all the good food they had wasted on him – the devil.

Jean shrugged. None of this concerned him. A little over a hundred years before, these rich people would have been put under a honed blade. That would have settled their minds wonderfully.

Ysabelle tossed between oblivion and awareness. She thought the pillow was Hāna, because some of Hāna's sweet scent had been left there. She thought the acid voluptuous aroma of the cherries, plucked by Mireio, or bleeding in the grass, was the sharp catch of Hāna's personal perfume in the moments of her ecstasy.

In her fever, Ysabelle spasmed in a deathly pleasure.

When the fever broke, pale and shuddering, Ysabelle sat by the window.

The nightingale still sang. She heard it all night long, as the swelling of her leg waned with the moon.

"No rain," said Mireio.

Seven days passed, and then Ysabelle went to her writing table, and began to try to compose a letter to Ernst. It was to be a love letter, confessing she could not bear not to see him. That his disapproval broke her heart. He had witnessed her ultimate foolishness, kissing his sister, locked in a female fantasy that Hāna was himself. Would he forgive her, come to her? She did not want marriage, never had, but to lose his regard – it burnt her away, like the summer leaves.

As she was writing this letter, over and over, attempting

to make it right, Ernst's letter to Ysabelle arrived, along with a package, its contents also wrapped over and over, in expensive paper from the city.

"My dear Friend," he began, "Ysabelle: I know what worry you must have endured, and as soon as the burden upon me was eased, I sat down to write to you. We both of us care for Hāna so deeply. Let me assure you at once that now the terrible insanity which overwhelmed her has been alleviated. Could you see her, as I did, two days ago, look into her face, clear of all shadow and every frightful thing, you would know, as I do, that this was for the best

"You will understand, that morning I calmed her as well as I might. Luckily, I keep some opiates by me, for use in certain of my experiments. These rendered Hāna her first peace, and after that I was able to convey her to St Cailloux. Here my friend, Le Ruc, took charge of her at once.

"She had by now awoken, and on feeling her pulse, which was so rapid, he declared immediately this was enough to inform him such a passionate heart was unnatural, and could do her only harm. He confided to me that, in the Dark Ages, she would have been supposed possessed by the Devil. But he is a man of science. The 'Devil' is merely in her mind, its disorder. He acted before nightfall.

"I will not describe to you the operation, the details might alarm you, and besides you would not understand it. It involves certain nerve fibres in the frontal portion of the brain. A delicate pruning away. My magnificent friend, he made the tender incision. He is adept, and although Hāna was his very first subject the success with her has made him sanguine for the help of others.

"It was a practice in Ancient Egypt studied by him closely. Curious to think, that when they lay Hāna in the tomb at last she too will bear this same scar upon her forehead and her skull, as did those persons in that land of pyramids.

"Ah, Ysabelle. Dear sister. If you could see her. She is like a little child again. Everything is new to her. The flight of a bird startles, even that. She does not move from her chair. A picture of repose, her drooping head, her folded hands. Le Ruc says she does not quite know me – I fear she would not know you at all. But when I ask her to smile for me, she does. She will be well cared for, there. And though I must soon be gone from this country, Le Ruc will take thought for her like his own. As indeed, he does for all his charges in that place.

"A note on my gift, which accompanies this letter. You will have realised, it is her hair, which of course, for such medical attention, had to be cut off entirely. All the shining locks. It seemed to me you might value them, dear Ysabelle, as you did when you were to her her closest and most intimate friend.

"Beyond this, my kindest wishes for your continued good health and the ending of your local drought.

"Your brother, if so I may call myself:

"Ernst."

In her diary, her Book, Ysabelle wrote, "I sent for the old man, the charcoal burner they call *Doggy*. Having given him some coins, he went for me to the place, which he names Wolf Valley. He was the only one I could trust. He, and his kind, keep away from the village. He has under his shirt an amulet, dried sticks twisted in a knot. Near dawn, he came back. He had said there he was an old servant and asked for her. Expectedly, they would not let him in, but said she was in the care of Dr Le Ruc, and he need have no fears. When Doggy said, as I told him to, that he hoped she was better, they laughed. He caught a glimpse of others, at some windows. Their heads were shaved. One was wrapped up tight and seemed to have no arms. The old man was brave. They hate that place."

Under this Ysabelle, or something, has scrawled in a

running jagged line:

Heart burst stifle and drown in blood.

Perhaps a curse, or a wish for self.

There are records from the asylum. One may see them, if the tactic is carried out properly. There is a note on a woman, called only by her Christian name, to 'protect' her. "Hāna, the prey of uncontrollable, obscene and perverse desires, a danger to herself and others." The operation, "The last possible resort", and "practised among the ancients", was a "success".

Before the final page, Ysabelle sets out for herself some instructions on how best to hang herself. The strong beam in the lower room that faces the afternoon glare of the mountains, and will hold her weight, which, she admits, is much less, as she cannot eat. Mireio and Jean will be sent away with a settlement of money, as the last page also explains. The hair, a dead thing, still with its stranded mauve ribbons that she herself had helped, that morning of the ending, to tie there, is to be strongly plaited, not as before; woven, not with silk, but some coarse twine, to make it sure. And she will be naked, lest the rigidity of her clothes impedes her.

Ysabelle understands, from her reading, that few people die quickly when hanged. They are choked and strangle. In this way, the hair will throttle her, and as she kicks and gags in instinctive physical panic, her soul will remember that it is Hāna who is killing her, as she has killed Hāna. She affirms she will wear the silver locket with Hāna's sexual hair. She has polished the metal.

She says, as if she has forgotten it was mentioned before, and as she says again, too, on the last page, that she has heard of a goat being sacrificed to bring rain.

After that, she says the nightingale has flown away.

Then she says she has finished.

After which, there is the last page.

There are some further pages after that, blank, obviously.

Inevitably, one fills them with the mind – the presumed hanging, the woman choking and kicking, rocked violently from side to side in the white vacant empty house, then only turning, slowing, still, a pendant, while the mountains and the sun stare in. After which, as it seems almost supernaturally, fire catches the house, and burns it to the ground, leaving only the puns – St Cailloux – of the lower stone floors and stone chimneys and the stone hearths, and the stone under which the book is, until the old man, maybe Doggy, fetches it out and brings it here, to me.

In a year's time, a peasant, travelling up the lane on foot, will pause by the ruin of the house. The land by then will have been sold off, but no one, as yet, come to restore or change it. The untended cherry trees will be leafy yet, although one or two will have succumbed to the ivy, with here and there a green young fruit hard among the foliage.

The man, a stranger, will not be troubled by any stories of the region, and going into the ruin, will poke about, since sometimes, in this way, he has found useful things others have overlooked. He will find, however, nothing, and so sit down by a stone, part of one, now collapsed, chimney. He will eat his olives and bread. Then he will fall asleep, for the sun will be again very hot.

When he wakes it will be to great alarm. Across from him, in the wild grass, a small fire will have started. He must leap up to put it out and do so quickly. For in this weather, another summer drought fire is the fiercest enemy.

This man is canny. When once he has dealt with the danger, he will find a soreness at his chest and looking down, where hangs the little silver cross given him as a boy he will come to see at once what has happened, for he has heard of it before.

An hour after, in the village, he will tell his tale over his wine and so unravel the mystery of Madame Ysabelle's house. The truth will not make any difference to her burial place, in fact will only consolidate her rights to holy ground, since no one has generally told the plan of suicide written in her diary.

Now they will say without compunction, that some object – glass, or mirror, carelessly left by the departing servants – caught the harsh light from the mountains, and cast it off in a ray against the wooden wall. The concentration of this burning-glass presently sent the tinder of the drought-dry house up in a conflagration.

Most of that will be true. Not quite all. For it was no picture or glass that caused the focus of an incendiary ray, the lighting of a death pyre. It was the polished silver locket that lay pendant on the breast of Ysabelle's hanged corpse, once she had stopped moving, once she hung quite still, a pendant herself, naked silver on a silver chain of hair, from the beam above.

I have a lock of your hair.
I cut
It from you as you slept.
I kissed you there,
Where
The scissors met.
You never noticed it had gone.
It is all I have of you,
Your hair.
Blonde spirals in
A silver locket.

Death Fell In Love with a Stuffed Marmoset in a Taxidermist's Store Front Window.

John Kaiine, with Tanith Lee

Death has always been very good to me. Y'see, I am Death's narrator. Just a normal, everyday bloke. Nothing special. It's just, we got to chatting once, some while ago and we just clicked, y'know. He seemed the lonely type and wanted to talk. I'm a good listener, so I'm told. So I listened. And listen still. I've learnt a lot, and if it helps him, so much the better. If not, well, I've got nothing better to do with my time. Time's all I got.

I must admit, I'm touched. For today, Death asked me to be his best man.

For Death fell in love with a stuffed marmoset in a taxidermist's store front window. Dunno where, or *when* it was, but he's happy. Silly as a schoolmaid. It's nice to see.

Sprightly, Death takes to wearing a cummerbund and Persian slippers. He sports now a dapper waxed moustache and effects an heroic limp.

Death makes a purchase – pays in cash, big notes, no plastic – doesn't want it gift-wrapped, pops it under his arm and strolls pridefully out. No one gives him a second glance – just Death carrying a stiff, grey black-furred, gloss-green glass-eyed primate down the street.

Once home, Death lights all the candles for a romantic little light supper and sets the world on fire.

I was proud to be there, to see the courtship begin – me out in the shadows looking on, peeling the veg,

To set the mood, Barry White B-sides are interspersed between stirring Communist state national anthems.

Dry sherry with ice. Plantains simmered in saffron.

Death has a light touch. And taste.

Inseparable, Death takes his marmoset love everywhere.

Wooing with afternoons out, punting on the Cam in torrential downpours. Long, warm nights stoking the embers of the Sanjo Palace. Laughing at their shadows in 4th Dynasty Egyptian twilight. Watching Somme sun-up knotted over with shrapnel and swallows.

How dreamy, the scent of magnolia and burning Greek galleys. What joy, to go skipping through late Renaissance courtyards.

Death does a modest dance. A macabre little tarantella. I've never seen him so happy.

Suddenly, giddy over a breakfast of kedgeree, down on one knee, delirious, Death proposes marriage.

The engagement of Death to his beloved marmoset is announced. It's in all the papers. Even the free ones.

Love. Even more than Death himself, love's the chaos-bringer, the quake, rocking the world, remaking things in its own image. The hardness of her form, in its slightly musty case of fur, sleek as a 50's *Dior* gown. The dark mask of her devilish face. To take her in his arms is like moonlight and wine. They can dance till dawn, and the dawn will wait for *them*. Death has come alive. I saw all that, through the glowing rainstorms and all those labyrinthine courtyards. RSVP Invitations are sent out from Delaware to Chittagong,

Death had a double portrait commissioned by an anonymous Flemish master.

The entire wedding breakfast is to be served from and upon Hohokam pottery.

Merchants thronged the silk routes, bringing exquisite silks, embroidery and moth-wing cloth.

The guests –among many were Mictlantecuhtli – Libitina – Valdis – Ah Puch – and, *let's suppose*, the surviving Kennedys.

The bride's maids to be dressed as characters from *Gone With The Wind.* The page boys – daubed in blue woad. Death himself plans on wearing a bullet-ridden Lakota Sioux Ghost Shirt and spats.

Me, I have many duties to oversee – for one, the speech. During which Death swore me on no account to mention his long held crush on Eve, or his arachnophobia. And especially never to admit that he still hadn't finished *that* 500 piece jigsaw.

Brass, the wedding ring is brass. A little curtain ring that Death picked up in the Doge's Palace, between plagues.

The music to be played exclusively upon a xylophone, cheekily fashioned entirely from chameleon bones.

The cake: he wants two. One, the Siege of Leningrad under thick white icing snow. The second – Krakatoa – lava red icing there.

The Limousine is to be pulled by a dozen white rhino. Of course.

He's already thinking of their future children's name – Ted, after his favourite poet. Solly? And for a girl – Berengaria, princess of Navarre, or, Rydal – the name of a very beautiful lake.

You really don't want to know about Death's stag-night…

Let's just say there's one less palaeontologist about and an awful lot more wilted rice paddies out there than there should be this morning.

Morning.

That morning it was all a blur.

The bridegroom pacing so eager, in awe of joy.

And then. All a blur. A handwritten note presented me by some superbly drab creature – male or female, don't ask me, I can't recall. And looking at this bloody note, all I can think is '*that's not how you spell Australia…*' I had to break the news – a whisper in Death's ear. His marmoset had 'received a better offer'.

Death has been jilted at the altar of their Las Vegas Casino wedding venue. By a handwritten note.

Y'know, she was something, his marmoset. Ever really looked at one? At one that's stuffed? Eyes to mend or break your heart. And the stuffy stiffness of that fur, the smell of sawdust, faintest stinging tang of formaldehyde. The little chips – emerald, dirt, must, brilliance – in the dull glass green eyes. He only has a photo booth snapshot of her now.

The marmoset had emigrated to Australia. Opted for a new, *easier* life as a doorstop in a nightclub for cross-dressing muscle-men. Sweaty false eyelashes and the stink of the crowd.

Numb, a heart dumb with dust, Death honeymoons alone in Death Valley. Between thumb and fore-finger he plucks each and every spine from each and every cactus there.

Death goes for a long walk.

Several weeks later ~

I got a postcard from Death. Postmark - Easter Island.

Ha! The old bastard!

Nostalgic, Death paints all the colours of a Rubik's cube black.

Death was abused as a boy.

Death gets a pen pal.

Death dodged the draft.

Death's eyes are flies.

Death grows lactating titties so that he may breast feed an abandoned baby Inuit girl. Watching her; the lump of life hunched over a moment which will never happen. He knows about those all right.

Tipsy on Dutch Gin, Death gate-crashes a private Mongolian Horse-Milk Vodka-tasting party and on the rebound disgraces himself with a llama.

Death goes blackberry-picking at the base of a smouldering South Sea's volcano.

Death cheats at checkers.

Death is *not* insured.

Picking all the daisies from Howard Carter's unkempt grave, Death strings them together, making a daisy chain which he proudly wears.

Death turns a boney hand to campanology, for no better reason, than he wants to perform his piss-poor impression of Charles Laughton (circa 1939).

Through teeth tight as a hawk's hips, Death goes whistling *Gershwin* out of tune (naturally) to a madman strapped into a strait-waistcoat, black from old dried blood, as the inmate squirms on the floor of his 1821 Bedlam padded cell.

Sulking, Death sprouts a tail and trips up the ghost of Charlie Chaplin.

But none of that helps.

In a fit of pique, Death reinvents the wheel and mows down most of the Fifteenth Century.

Death farts at the opera.

Death misses his Mum.

Death would much rather be a hare.

Swathing himself in a swaddling blanket, Death clambers into a wicker cradle on the steps of an orphanage in downtown Prague. He is still there, unattended to at midnight. The hoarfrost gently settling.

Death dabbles in bi-sexuality, but doesn't much like the taste.

Taking a drag on a discarded cheroot, Death coughs up a long forgotten lung.

Foregoing stilt-walking, Death opts for a correspondence course in mastering the gentlemanly art of the Penny Farthing.

We can find Death today or yesterday practicing cross-stitch whilst hanging with his homies in a Guatemalan crack house.

Death shaves his legs.

Death fosters a particular fondness for prunes.

But nothing helps.

Nothing

Snoozy, Death is channel-zapping on the motel TV. The remote – click after click, again and again… CNN. Friendly fire. Industrial espionage. National Geographic Existence bullied down to the convenience of history. Nil-by-mouth cannibals, mid-life crisis M.I.L.F's and punch-drunk wrestlers. Parasites on the surface layer. Weekend Harley wannabe's. M.T. fucking V. The Weather Channel. Suits, smiles and tans, big hair, big fake tits and big fake hand-on-heart, attention-seeking emotional studio debates. Adverts for cars and pieces of finely sliced and diced dead animal. Adverts for chemicals. Adverts for adverts. Coming soon – a series devoted entirely to *Kitty Litter*. Roaring, Death throws the television out the window. Rock N' Roll – he'll show 'em! He paces the bland room, making a list, a new list. A *long* list.

Who's that over there in the shadows, there, on platform 3, *Rambuteau*, Paris Metro? – why, it's my old mate, Death, feeding candy-cotton by hand to the escaped hyenas.

Don't tell anyone, but Death dreams of chipped green eyes. Of fur the colour of Victorian mourning.

Death joins the circus. Sequins suit Death.

Waking up after a particularly raucous Ibizan weekend of Sushi, Karaoke, E and Tequila slammers, Death discovers a heart-shaped tattoo on his right tibia, emblazoned with the names 'Mindy' and 'Sanchez'.

Mindy?

Sanchez?

Ibiza!

He hurriedly packs, fleeing the island, deciding to lay low in the Sahara for the next decade or two.

Death cannot quite get his head around the concept of Steam Punk. But *really* likes the goggles. They help shut things out, maybe.

Atop this mountain now, only tattered black flags and the elation of temporary emptiness. Death likes it here, can just sit and be, thinking of his long lost, little, stuffed, green glossy-glassy-eyed primate love and what they ought to have been to one another, and all that they would never be. Two could have equalled One. They could have reinvented everything. But dreams and hopes – gone. Taken off: overseas, propping open a door for female-impersonating, steroid junkies. Ain't it always the way.

From the corner of one eye he sees Samurai and shaman drowning in old jungle ponds of cherry blossom. Worms, medals, Voodoo effigies, leaking from every obscene corner of sight. He blinks them away.

Death digs at his ear with a shark's tooth, at the white

noise of crooning magpies stripping flesh off architects' daughters. Deaths flicks at the din absentmindedly, as one would a mayfly.

He picks up mountain mud and rolls it in his hands, finding it has the texture of cellulite.

Death scratches his arse.

Upwind, he catches the whiff of wombs, bowels, bloated underbellies, ribbon-wrapped and blood warm, pumping out nests of Russian doll carrion. Finding another ant-hill, Death changes seats.

Death sucks his thumb and can taste ancient Rome and eggs over easy. He gobs out empires.

The black flags wrap him. Some warmth at least.

Beyond the mountain he's years ago, in the mad primitive forest, and up there, sudden as Death himself, he sees her. His marmoset. She was peeling and eating a little fruit in the nylon black mittens of her paws. She was living, then. She looked at him with eyes – not of green glass – but clear amber optical tissue. She didn't know him, never knew they'd meet when she was dead, and stuffed, and in a store window. Didn't know that they'd be everything to each other, for a little while. And now, well, she only turns her furry back and springs away. Death picks up discarded fruit peal, but it means nothing. She was and is too young for him back then. He didn't fancy her.

Death runs for the future, the present, the long lost past, *anywhere* but here.

Later, maybe before –

Super glam, Death becomes a successful catwalk model – all cheek bones and spindly.

Death auditions for a Goth band, but is laughed out of the studio for being far too Old-Skool.

Death dips a skeletal toe in the Red Sea and gets nipped by a Hermit Crab.

Tying the shoe laces of a matador together, Death sits back and waits…

Death has a lisp.

Halloween – Death dons a surgeon's gown and mask. While trick-or-treating chances upon a young lady writhing in an alleyway in the throes of labour. Well-skilled in such matters, Death assists, till with final scream – the mother's – her son is born. She gazes up, unseeing, eyes full of tear, asking, in whatever language, 'Oh, Doctor, can I name my baby after you?'

He doesn't say, What about Ted, or Solly? What about Berengaria, or Rydal? That fellow, Death, I hear he now distrusts names, *and* aerodynamics.

Ravenous, Death wants a doughnut. A big, juicy, glazed, white chocolate doughnut with caramel sauce and sprinkles. Death is greedy sometimes.

Death is haunted by the ghost of a Tandoori'ed cat. (Sad old Punjab memory).

Once, Death had an imaginary friend. It hanged itself.

Death is always smiling. Such pearly gnashers. *All the better to eat you with.*

Death lost his keys.

Death lost his heart.

Death has no alibi. There were plenty of witnesses.

At the water's edge, Death pens an inky suicide note and feigns his own demise – robes, hourglass, scythe discarded amongst the crumbling 1888 A.D seaside sand-castles. Taking a horse and carriage to the station, he boards the first locomotive. By evening he is in the late twentieth century: Northern Hemisphere. (Eastern Standard Time.) He takes to growing long, lank hair, dresses down with plaits, sandals and guitar – a gaunt, backpacking hippy to any that chanced to look. He sings, badly, about green eyes, nylon mittens, bitten fruit.

Death leaves a Mother-of-Pearl button, two Laundromat tokens and a Spanish Doubloon in his empty soup-kitchen bowl. Death is a generous tipper. Can afford to be.

Death always cuts the crusts off his bread and butter – he doesn't want curly hair.

Death, most certainly, does not Blog.

Death will not take an I.O.U.

Don't offer one.

And… Never ask Death directions.

On an impulse, Death buys a mauve lycra thong, but swiftly regrets it, returning it for some *Tidy Whities.*

Death imagines himself the dandy police inspector in a saucy 19th Century murder mystery. Death likes corsets. But they're often furry black.

Begrudgingly, Death writes his will and leaves his unworldly goods to all of the sunflowers, thorns and nettles. Though not to the lilies of the field. Apparently they get a private income.

Lolling languid in a hammock on a nuclear submarine, blowing big, bright pink *Bazooka Joe* bubbles, Death re-reads Jung and doodles in the margins. Sketches of marmosets.

Death searches frenziedly for a certain *something*; he looks and looks in every last room and chamber of the Palace of Versailles, but cannot find it.

Death has new neighbours. They keep him awake with their vigorous sexual grunts and animalistic moans. They didn't invite him to their house-warming party. They have a yappy dog and one spotty son.

Death gets caught shoplifting in *Walmart.* Oh, the shame! First Treblinka, then Ibiza, now this! To avoid attention, he dons a disguise of *Way-Fearers*, cheap, white plastic vampire teeth and a dubiously-acquired quiz-show host's toupée.

Bored and breathing on a steamed-up church stained-glass window, passer-by Death draws on to it, with one dull knuckle bone, a little stick figure with an over-exaggerated thick stick penis and balls. The church doors are barred. The church and its shrieking congregation are all burning. Soldiers with machetes and AK47's look on from the bush.

Death has always been very good to me.

It's never boring when Death's about!

Originally? It was a strange drawing together, a mutual attraction, if you will. Think of me as a silent partner.

My name? Oh, didn't I say… It's Life.

Life is Death's narrator.

Life was Death's best man.

Death has always been extremely patient with me, too. He taught me a lot – explained what immortality was all about. It took me a while, but yeah, I'm getting used to it.

We've knocked about a bit, me and Death. There was this very memorable occasion; it cracked us up – I was there, but didn't *actually* observe what happened. Y'see, I was in one of the many resplendent marble bathrooms trying to take a dump at the time – but I did *hear* the altercation outside – Seems Death had told Grigori Yefimovich Rasputin that 'его язык имел дерьмо и алмазы на этом…*' All I can say is it's a good thing we were wearing snow-shoes…

*(General translation) ~ *His tongue had shit and diamonds on it…*

Torn and trembling, Death has no appetite for a gladiator's turd, a sailor's stitched lips, the wept and weeping. Rhyme and rottenness, no *reason* for reason, every last thing, maggot, man, moon, must die.

Lonesome, Death licks rust from the long-locked-up,

barred and shuttered door of his favourite NY salt-beef sandwich bar – Lower East Side, East Houston, corner of Ludlow.

Death drop-kicks a strapismic encyclopedia salesman in Minnesota; gentle rain, autumn, 1964. Just because.

Death rides a pale horse – a clapped out, mottled, grey, knackers' yard nag. Rides it side saddle, he does. Like a big girl.

Death avoids Wall Street and Area 51 in exchange for racing tips and fresh-baked Baklava.

Hotwiring a classic 1951 (scarlet and cream) Mercury coupé, Death takes a spin on a Sunday afternoon, wolf-whistling aboriginal strangers in the Outback.

Death gets a tan and a speeding ticket too.

Disillusioned, Death becomes a Buddhist.

Nothing helps.

Death has a shadow-puppet fetish.

That doesn't help either.

Watch and listen as Death sits with the remains of some hastily-unearthed, scabby, Mummy-wrapped Aztec on his knee, using it as a ventriloquist's doll to commune with the ashes and crumbs of the indiscreet mistresses of Byzantine royalty. They tell him nothing he doesn't know.

Johannesburg: New Year's Day – Death beats an umbrella-seller to a pulp for treading on cracks in the sidewalk. Death shoots his cuffs, clicks his neck, walks on through deep, dark puddles. Fur dark. Neon green.

Raging from an imagined literary slight, Death sours to jealous and reworks Greek mythology. Death rapes Oedipus, sniffs and pockets Jocasta's warm, worn under-slip, hides Charon's oars, spikes Dionysus's drink, tars and feathers Icarus, engages the Cyclops in an abnormally grotesque game of Blind-Man's-Buff, kicks Kronos in the cobblers, and gives an enema of scalding clay to the Minotaur.

Wrapped up warm, Death builds a snowman as the first bombs drop.

Death catches a chill and takes to his bed.

Death sent out for pizza, but it never arrived.

Does anything, really?

Death peels an orange and then peels an onion. He can tell no difference.

Death skulks, picking his teeth in Hamilcar's overgrown garden.

Death failed all his Rorschach tests.

Death forgets. Death forgets how to forget.

Death laughs. He likes a good laugh, does Death.

Laughs at the non-stop herds of sheeple. Guffaws at those cute kitten cartoons in the Sunday funny papers too. Chuckles his way through another Super 8mm film of atrophied trophy wives, beheaded, yet sucking and swallowing still.

Glancing on, laughing, up a tree while a parade of African elephants trample an ivory poacher into the ground.

Hee hee.

Floating about, looking in at one more open-mouthed astronaut, Death can only snigger. Even though some of those stars burn green.

As all the tele-prompters fail, Death rejoices in the knowledge that last words do not count.

Memories of the Passage of Khourd Caboul massacre find him in paroxysms of laughter.

When the virgin sacrifice is discovered to be not all she appears to be…

Death laughs and laughs and laughs.

And don't even get him started on sweat shops and salt mines.

No, don't. *Really.*

Death cries too.

For Death knows.

Cries for those locked in *that* cupboard, reported missing. Cries as the last ones won't be coming back.

Cries.

For fell and failed and those little flies trapped in amber.

Gulping down tears and snot for two pairs of lovers' shoes left outside an afternoon hotel door; Death does not understand DO NOT DISTURB.

He bites his own tongue, does Death – volcanic sobs that flood away the bacteria and dust of all eternities' quiet decay. Laments for each and every incident between instance.

Cries as forgotten tin soldiers corrode, their gaudy painted colours flaking. Weeps for shadows unseen and blubs over misspelled fortune cookies.

He knows.

He *is* the punch-line. The 8 Ball carved of bone.

In grief, lurched over, Death cries and cries and cries for his darling marmoset.

Death blows his nose on a white flag of surrender.

Death learns to enjoy keeping honey bees in rural Sussex and keeps *himself* to himself. I visit him there and see he has swapped his dowdy hood for an Edwardian bee-keeper's mask.

Death and I sipped home-made mead into the wee small hours. Those little bats circling us. We talked about our old times together: when he took me to see the wet-finger-daubed, red ochre paintings of bulls on the walls of the caves in Lascaux, and how we had front row seats watching the Pittsburgh Pirates lose the first ever World Series. Going souvenir-hunting in Marrakech and drunkenly defacing the walls of old Pompeii. And who could forget the birth of Albrecht Durer and the Lisbon passing of Queen Catherine of Braganza. Happy times we had. But it's silly of me, I still can't recollect where we first met – some swamp, I think. I do, however, recall that it was very, *very* dark.

Later:

And he paid for my cab fare home.

We waved and waved our then goodbyes.

I never saw Death again.

He was always very good to me. Treated me like a brother. No, much better than any brother.

Y'know, I have no idea what I'm going to do without him.

I really will miss him. *The old bastard.*

For Death grew wings and flew away. It was all a mistake.

All a mistake.

Mills

Publishing History

'Arborium' – unpublished and original to this collection

'The Occasional Table', 2007 – unpublished and original to this collection.

'Torhec the Sculptor' – *Asimov's Magazine*, (Ed. Sheila Williams), 2010.

'Doll Re Mi' – Electronic publication, *Nightmare Magazine*, (Ed. John Joseph), 2012.

'A House on Fire' – *Haunts: Reliquaries of the Dead*, (Ed. Steven Jones), Ulysses Press, 2011.

'Eva Beneath the Serpent Tree', 1977 (approx) – unpublished and original to this collection.

'La Dame' – *Sisters of the Night,* (Ed. Barbara Hambly and Martin H. Greenberg), Time Warner, 1996.

'The Pretty Knife', 2011 – unpublished and original to this collection.

'The Bench', 2013 – unpublished and original to this collection.

'Unlocked' (with John Kaiine) – *The Mammoth Book of New Terror*, (Ed. Stephen Jones), Robinson 2004.

'Death Fell in Love with a Stuffed Marmoset in a Taxidermist's Store Front Window (with John Kaiine) 2012 – unpublished and original to this collection.

About the Author

Tanith Lee was born in North London (UK) in 1947 and died on 24th May 2015 at the age of 67. Because her parents were professional dancers (ballroom, Latin American) and had to live where the work was, she attended a number of truly terrible schools, and didn't learn to read – she was also dyslectic – until almost age 8. And then only because her father taught her. This opened the world of books to Lee, and by 9 she was writing. After much better education at a grammar school, Lee went on to work in a library. This was followed by various other jobs – shop assistant, waitress, clerk – plus a year at art college when she was 25-26. In 1974 this mosaic ended when DAW Books of America, under the leadership of Donald A Wollheim, bought and published Lee's *The Birthgrave*, and thereafter 26 of her novels and collections.

Since then Lee wrote over 90 books, and approaching 300 short stories. 4 of her radio plays have been broadcast by the BBC; she also wrote 2 episodes (*Sarcophagus* and *Sand*) for the TV series *Blake's 7*. Some of her stories regularly feature on Radio 7.

Lee wrote in many styles in and across many genres, including Horror, SF and Fantasy, Historical, Detective, Contemporary-Psychological, Children and Young Adult. Her preoccupation, though, was always people.

In 1992 she married the writer-artist-photographer John Kaiine, her companion since 1987. They lived and worked together on the Sussex Weald, near the sea, in a house full of books and plants, with two black and white overlords called cats.

About the Artist

Jarod Mills is an artist and musician, who lives and works in St. Paul, MN. He played guitar in the metal band Epicurean from 2005 to 2009. For art inquiries find him on Facebook or email him at jarodmills2020@hotmail.com.

Allison Rich

Daughter of the Night was created by Jim Pattison and Paul Soanes in Toronto, Canada in 1990 or early 1991. It made its appearance on the Internet in 1996.

I must have discovered the bibliography when I got my first computer in 1995. Having discovered the works of Tanith Lee in 1986, my first year at university, I contacted Jim and offered my services in locating ongoing and past publications for the bibliography.

Jim was ready to give up the bibliography in 2003 for several reasons. It had been such a help to me over the years – and to other fans of her work – and it took me only a month to decide to take it over from him. After all, I am a librarian and used to working with enumerative bibliographies in my capacity as a rare books cataloguer. Jim wrote me that he had been hoping that *I* would be the one who would email him and volunteer to assume responsibility for the care and feeding of the bibliography. The files were transferred to me via CD-ROM and I registered the URL for *Daughter of the Night.*

Since 2003 I have toiled faithfully in order to make it the most comprehensive bibliography of the works of Tanith Lee. It was my idea to index the foreign translations. In the 13 years I have maintained it, I have had the help of Tanith's fans all over the world, who have sent me her books in other languages, or who have alerted me to something that was lacking. While I get the credit for the bibliography, *Daughter of the Night* is truly a group effort, which I always strive to point out to anyone who believes I have primary responsibility for the work!

Tanith emailed me to introduce herself sometime in 2003. In 2004, I met Tanith at Octocon in Dublin and we became friends. I would go and see her nearly every year, and stay in Hastings for a few days, until November of 2015. A few years before she died, as we sat in The Stag in Hastings, over a Sunday roast, she asked me to be the guardian of her literary legacy. Of course, I said yes. It is my honor and privilege and, moreover, my duty to all her fans around the world.

Daughter of the Night has, in the end, become exactly what I envisioned: *the* official Tanith Lee bibliography on the internet. I intend to maintain it for many years to come. Please consider it to be *the* source for her writings and secondary literature about her writings. Moreover if you see something which is lacking by all means, please email me!

Allison Rich
Webmistress of *Daughter of the Night*
www.daughterofthenight.com
Rhode Island, USA

(Allison Rich's contact information is on the *Daughter of the Night* web site.)

Books by Tanith Lee

A Selection from her 96 titles

The Birthgrave Trilogy (The Birthgrave; Vazkor, son of Vazkor, Quest for the White Witch)
The Vis Trilogy (The Storm Lord; Anackire; The White Serpent)
The Flat Earth Opus (Night's Master; Death's Master; Delusion's Master; Delirium's Mistress; Night's Sorceries)
Don't Bite the Sun
Drinking Sapphire Wine
The Paradys Quartet (The Book of the Damned; The Book of the Beast; The Book of the Dead; The Book of the Mad)
The Venus Quartet (Faces Under Water; Saint Fire; A Bed of Earth; Venus Preserved)
Sung in Shadow
A Heroine of the World
The Scarabae Blood Opera (Dark Dance; Personal Darkness; Darkness, I)
The Blood of Roses
When the Lights Go Out
Heart-Beast
Elephantasm
Reigning Cats and Dogs
The Unicorn Trilogy (Black Unicorn; Gold Unicorn; Red Unicorn)
The Claidi Journals (Law of the Wolf Tower; Wolf Star Rise, Queen of the Wolves, Wolf Wing)
The Piratica Novels (Piratica 1; Piratica 2; Piratica 3)
The Silver Metal Lover
Metallic Love
The Gods Are Thirsty

Collections

Nightshades
Dreams of Dark and Light
Red As Blood – Tales From the Sisters Grimmer
Tamastara, or the Indian Nights
The Gorgon
Tempting the Gods
Hunting the Shadows
Sounds and Furies

Also Published by Immanion Press

The Colouring Book Series

Greyglass
To Indigo
L'Amber
Killing Violets (Gods' Dogs)
Ivoria
Cruel Pink
Turqoiselle

Other Titles

A Different City
Ghosteria 1: the Stories
Ghosteria 2: the novel: Zircons May Be Mistaken
Legenda Maris

By John Kaiine

Fossil Circus

CPSIA information can be obtained
at www.ICGtesting.com
Printed in the USA
LVHW111621190822
726377LV00005B/505